What the press says about Harlequin Romances...

"...clean, wholesome fiction...always with an upbeat, happy ending."
—*San Francisco Chronicle*

"...a work of art."
—*The Globe & Mail*, Toronto

"Nothing quite like it has happened since *Gone With the Wind*..."
—*Los Angeles Times*

"...among the top ten..."
—*International Herald-Tribune*, Paris

"Women have come to trust these clean, easy-to-read love stories about contemporary people, set in exciting foreign places."
—*Best Sellers*, New York

OTHER
Harlequin Romances
by JOYCE DINGWELL

Remember September

by

JOYCE DINGWELL

Harlequin Books

TORONTO • LONDON • NEW YORK • AMSTERDAM • SYDNEY

Original hardcover edition published in 1977
by Mills & Boon Limited

ISBN 0-373-02189-5

Harlequin edition published August 1978

CHAPTER ONE

Paddy (christened Padua) put down the paper and went to stand at the window of her fifteenth floor bed-sit. From this height the roar of the traffic came muted and not un-attractive, the dust and grime of industry less distasteful, but descend a few flights, Paddy grimaced, and all that goes with a concrete jungle would enclose you again, you would be prisoner once more in a big city.

However, all that was over now ... or soon would be; the unpolluted bliss of country life was about to enfold her instead. Paddy had the frankly surprising evidence of this in the form of a just-opened letter on the table behind her, indeed she had actually started to hug herself in glee when Jerry's advertisement had caught her eye. Dear Jerry, she had smiled fondly at once, so he was still remembering after twelve hectic months.—Yes, they certainly would have been hectic, as hers had been, for at twenty racing helter-skelter to twenty-one, life is like that.

Paddy traced the busy passage of a beetling bus in the teeming street below and wondered how Jerry looked now that he, like she, had come of age. Yet somehow she could not picture Jerry any older, she could not imagine him caught up in maturity, he had been so fresh, so naïve, so much the eternal elf, the constant sprite. She

5

had even told him so once, she recalled, had said he would never grow old, but his face had clouded so completely she had added soothingly that she wished that she anyway could remain in spring.

Spring! It was spring again now, Down Under September, the first month of the Australian breakthrough, when fat buds burst and blossoms froth out, and Jerry, that eternal elf, that constant sprite, was saying in an advertisement:

'Maryrose, Remember September? Magnus.'

'Yes, Magnus,' Paddy smiled aloud, 'I remember.'

It had been at Pelican Beach on the far north coast, a bitten-in bay with yellow sand, lapping tides, a smell of fish, a cottage with a caretaker, an exclusive camping ground, and little else. Paddy had been given a loan of a friend's tent and tent-site on the exclusive ground so as to have a quiet spot to study for her finals. Jerry's reason to be at Pelican ... he had been in the one cottage ... had been rather the same, Paddy had gathered, if vaguely, for a subject as prosaic as study very soon had been well down on both their lists.

Yes, precious little revision the pair of them had done, she recalled, and she had meant precious in another way as well, for it had been a very precious period.

Not sentimentally precious, not even nostalgically so, just two young people coming together and forming an instinctive friendship, liking to do the same things at the same time, not needing to talk but when they did talk, talking eagerly, easily and with laughter.

'You're the best damn mate a fellow could ask, old man,' Jerry had praised. He often called her old man.

'You're the nicest idiot I've met,' Paddy had returned.

'Tch, tch, such love talk!' Jerry had grinned. 'But I

6

mean it, old man. I've never had a friend. I didn't have enough time at school to collect one. I was considered delicate, ho-ho, so I had lessons at home.'

'And now you're taking your deprivation out on me.'

'I think you're enjoying it as much as I am.'

'It's fine so long as it doesn't set me back in the exam,' Paddy had pointed out.

'You were only chewing over old lessons, anyway, the break will do you good, clear your head.'

'Yours, too.'

'I haven't any.'

'Head?' Paddy queried.

'I really meant brains in it. Big Brother got them.'

'Oh, so you have that trouble, too,' Paddy had groaned.

She had told Jerry about her two sisters, both doctors, then about the third little pig in the family, herself, who had only received half their grey matter.

'So,' she had finished, 'I've taken this less grey matter course.'

'Tell me about it again. Sort of housemother, isn't it?'

'I do dream at times that I will eventually become Matron, but that would be years away and I'd have to have a comfortable bosom first.'

'Never you, old man,' Jerry had grinned.

'It's practical nursing, practical cooking, practical psychology and a smattering of teaching all mixed up together to comprise a new diploma,' she explained. 'After you graduate, you do day stuff for years, then one morning, heigh ho, you're given a family of your own.'

'Without marriage lines?'

'With hard work and application, dopey,' Paddy had said.

'Also that comfortable bosom.'

'Probably, but once I'm through my finals I'm going to apply for every vacancy, bosom or not, with the hope that at last the C.F.A.—Closer Families Association—recommend me, if only to stop seeing my name.'

'The name of Paddy,' Jerry had nodded.

'Actually Padua. My parents loved Padua when they were in Italy ... cathedrals, ancient bridges, arcades. Of course I hated it. Girls mostly hate their names. I always yearned to be called Maryrose.'

'Why?'

'It's pretty. Didn't you want a different name?'

'You bet. Magnus.'

'That means great.'

'Which I'm not.' Jerry had given his rather thin shoulders a resigned hunch. A little abruptly, Paddy had regretted, for she would have liked to have heard more, he had dropped the subject to challenge instead : 'I'll race you to the buoy. Last out of the water buys the lunch.'

—That had been the kind of September to be remembered; it had been ... casual bits and pieces about families but nothing intimate—why, they hadn't even bothered to learn each other's surnames, it had been either Paddy and Jerry, or old man and mate, and occasionally ... as in the ad ... Maryrose and Magnus.

They had fished together, prawned together, climbed a headland together, sailed together, then one evening Jerry had said :

'Thirty days hath September, and tomorrow I'm expected home.'

'I'm expected, too. It's been great. I hope you pass your exam.'

'My exam ... Oh, yes. And I hope you get a comfortable bosom.'

At the bus the next morning they had grinned good-bye to each other. Later Jerry had bought Paddy a paper at the station to read on the Sydney train; he lived inland from Pelican Beach and would be home hours before she would, he said.

'I always look at the P. and M.F.,' he had told her of the paper.

'P. and M.F.?' she queried.

'Personal and Missing Friends—the agony coloumn. Have a look, old man, there might be one in for us.'

'Don't be silly!'

'Well, there will be next year. You watch for it. 'Bye now, Pad, and thanks.'

He had gone one way, she had gone another. Because of the name omission she'd never found out about his exam ... nor he, she grinned, about her comfortable bosom, lack of. But she had passed quite well, though little good it had done for her. As Mr Aston, the Principal of Closer Families Association, had said, in a calling like this it was age and experience that the Board looked for, not high marks—why, some of the wards to be house-mothered might be almost the same age as Paddy herself, and that would never do, my dear.

'You must be patient and wait,' he had advised.

'Until I have a comfortable bo——' Paddy had almost finished for him, and she had wished she had had Jerry beside her to giggle with her.

Well, she hadn't had him, but evidently she did now in spirit. Who else but Jerry would have inserted:

'Maryrose, Remember September? Magnus.'

So that eternal elf, that constant sprite had not grown up after all ... just as she hadn't, and Mr Aston had been rather pessimistic about that.

'Maturity is what counts most. Now take this latest assignment. It's really quite an important position, Padua, but you look—well——'

Paddy had gulped at what he had not said but had still prompted: 'The position, Mr Aston?'

'A place called Yoothamurra. Very apt, don't you think?'

'Apt?' she asked.

'The name is aboriginal and fits its purpose perfectly. But of course, you'd already know about that, knowing, as everyone must know, about Yoothamurra.'

Paddy had *not* known but had not said so. In this game of getting a job you never missed a trick, you never let on that you were unknowledgeable.

'The successful house-mother to this Closer Family,' Mr Aston had continued, 'will be taking over a large home in the far north coast.'

'Yoothamurra?'

'Yes. The patron, a wealthy person, has divided up his substantial residence, one side for the wards and their supervisor, the other side for himself, but he will be constantly in attendance, and since he has donated extremely generously will naturally expect only the best. I'm not implying that you're not that, Padua dear, not the best in learning, but——'

'No bosom ... I mean, not experienced enough, Mr Aston?'

'I hardly think so. And yet——'

'And yet?'

Mr Aston had not answered that, instead he had advised: 'So even though I'm telling you to apply, don't despair when——'

When she had picked up the letter a few minutes ago,

Paddy, seeing its source, *had* despaired. Almost she had not bothered to open it, then—well, she had.

'Dear Miss Travis, Re Closer Families Association appointment, I hereby inform you that you have been successful in your application for the job of housemother at Yoothamurra.

'If you will call at the above office you will receive particulars as to salary, commencement date, receive your transit ticket, the rest.

'Yours, etc.

'M. David.'

It had been a brief intimation but quite sufficient. About to hug herself with joy, Paddy had seen the *Herald*, an old one, she noted, evidently by the brown stains on it wrapped around the potatoes, and she had read the ad and for a short moment forgotten her heady success.

'Maryrose, Remember September? Magnus.'

Oh, yes, she remembered, and she even blew a careless kiss to the paper, the kind of kiss an old man would give to a nice idiot ... or would an old man and a nice idiot?

But there were other things to be done now, there was her future to be considered. Matron of Yoothamurra! Paddy tasted it deliciously. Or Yoothamurra Housemother? Not so impressive but quite satisfactory. She wondered what Yoothamurra meant.

But immediately she must ring her sisters and tell them. She must give the landlord notice. She must inform Mr Aston. Most important of all, she must present herself at the city office of this person called M. David.

'So, Magnus,' Paddy said regretfully to the paper, 'you'll understand, won't you, if I don't spend much time remembering this year? How are you, Magnus? Successful? Starting to get a little pompously paunchy now? On the verge of being married? Or even' ... a giggle ... 'already a fond papa, for you would have had time.'

Laughing at her nonsense, Paddy took up the phone and dialled the office of M. David and was answered at once by M. David's secretary.

Yes, Paddy agreed with the secretary, she could commence promptly. Yes, that salary was fine. Yes, she could call tomorrow for her ticket. Yes, she would sign the agreement then. Yes, yes, yes.

Waiting in the city office of Mr M. David ... what was the function of the office? ... the next day, while the secretary attended to the ticket and finished preparing the agreement, Paddy, crossing to a large map on the wall, located her future place of employment. It was on the far north coast of New South Wales, as Mr Aston had said, but in the hinterland section of it. Paddy read Timber, Dairying, Bananas and Blood Stock beside a pencilled Yoothamurra that someone had rendered more prominent by an asterisk also in pencil.

Finished with that, Paddy glanced eastward on the map and of all places found Pelican Beach. Why, the two, Yoothamurra and Pelican, were quite close. Probably Jerry knew this M. David, Paddy thought.

'Mr David,' the secretary was saying, 'is up on the property.'

'Property?' asked Paddy.

'It's an extremely beautiful part of the state. I think the wards are very fortunate in that, if in nothing else.'

'Are they one family?' The policy of the Board was to keep an orphaned or deserted family together, and Paddy's lectures had mostly been slanted that way.

'No, four loners. Well, sometimes it does happen that

way. People do have only children. But you'll soon learn the rest when you get there, which will be——?' The secretary had looked inquiringly at Paddy.

'Tomorrow. Or is that too soon?'

'I think it will be very satisfactory. Sign there, please, Miss Travis. The wards are already established, and as he's not a family man, I mean not married, I believe Mr David will be more than glad to see you.'

'Until he does see me.' Paddy had not been able to stop herself saying that.

'What, Miss Travis?'

'Well, I don't look ... well——'

'Experienced?' helped the secretary indulgently.

'Yes.'

'But Mr David would know that already. He chose you himself.'

'Chose me?' Paddy queried.

'Especially. I should know, I was directed to contact your Mr Aston ... is that right?'

'Yes, but Mr Aston never told me.'

'Probably remembered there's many a slip, so kept quiet in case you might be disappointed.'

'Yes, that would be Mr Aston,' appreciated Paddy. 'But—chose me?' She said it in honest puzzlement. Why would anyone choose inexperience when——

'There you are, then. Your ticket is booked on the Northern Mail. You alight at Turnabout Creek ... don't forget to warn the guard at the previous stop, as there's no staff at the conditional stop station. You'll be picked up from there by a Yoothamurra car. Goodbye, and good luck, Miss Travis, and don't look so puzzled. I know if it were me I would be *very* pleased to be *particularly* selected by *Mr David*.'

'Particularly selected?'

'I assure you.'

'Then I will be pleased.' But Paddy said it faintly. Why had anyone picked her?

But there had been no time to worry about it, there had only been time for the last essentials, then attendance at Central Railway at eight sharp the next morning.

The train had left on time, in more time again had lost the suburbs, rimmed the coast to Newcastle, then done the usual railway unrolling of hills, flats, woods and towns. Cows were followed by pigs and pigs by crops. In the afternoon the big timber started, and, late afternoon, the bananas.

At dusk the mail pulled up at the conditional stop of Turnabout Creek and everyone ... save Paddy ... came to the window to look out. Paddy was intent on getting out.

There was a raised platform of earth and a small shelter in case of rain, but nothing else. Trees closed in on either side, and in the dusky blue of early evening they came almost like a green explosion.

It seemed lush country, the kind of country that bounteous rainfalls and bounteous sun produce together. Paddy could name a lot of the trees at a glance ... silky oak, black walnut, silver ash. There were occasional banana intruders, too, only to be expected in banana terrain, and parasitic fig, wild orchids and liana vines hanging in Tarzan-inviting loops and swings.

Lastly, and just now most important, there was a big black car halted on a rough timber track. A man was sitting behind the wheel waiting for her, and his look, even from the distance of the platform, was hard, flinty and unwavering.

Paddy still stood where the guard had deposited both her and her bag on the bare earth rise with its sign Turnabout Creek, Advise Driver, but *her* look back was soft, yielding and wavering—wavering with emotion. Why, Jerry, she was rejoicing, Jerry after twelve months. Jerry who was 'mate' to her own 'old man', Magnus to her Maryrose. Her fellow twenty-year-old one green September ago.

'Remember September!' Paddy was laughing aloud as she bounded from the platform and ran to the car. Jerry *had* matured after all, she thought, he was not that sprite any more, but on the other hand he was not paunchy or anything like that.

He was getting out of the car now, and Paddy was pausing. Jerry ... yet not Jerry ... somehow not even Jerry, then. So—someone else?

'Magnus?' she said uncertainly.

'Yes, madam, Magnus David. I presume you are' ... a pause as he checked on a paper ... 'Miss Travis. Padua Travis.' Another ... significant? ... pause. 'Alias Maryrose.'

Paddy added jerkily, nonsensically: 'And old man.'

He did not comment on that. He said: 'Kindly be seated in the car, Miss Travis. It's getting dark, and as you can guess there are no lights on these smaller tracks, so we won't waste time. I'll fetch your bag.'

He had gone before his last word, a bigger, broader man than she had judged Jerry would grow into, very like Jerry, in fact the same, yet—yet——

'Brothers.' The man had returned now and put her bag in the back seat. 'That's to put you out of your misery of uncertainty,' he added.

'No misery,' Paddy assured him.

'But much memory?' he insinuated drily. 'It seemed so on Jeremy's part, anyway. Well, all that's finished now.' He had got in the car by now, and he began to move forward at once.

'You mean because I've been found?' asked Paddy confused. She had never dreamed that that September had meant such a lot to Jerry, it hadn't to her, it—it had just happened, it had just been good fun.

'No.' The man beside her negotiated a difficult bend rendered more difficult still because it twined between two spreading gums. 'No ... because Jerry now won't be inserting any more ads.'

'You mean—Remember September?' Paddy asked.

'Yes.'

'Jerry has married?' Yes, that would be it. Come to think of it, as a new wife she wouldn't very much care about it herself.

'No,' Magnus David answered harshly. 'Because he died.'

He began to climb, and though the going was rocky, he took enough time from his task to look quickly at Paddy and repeat himself.

'Jeremy is dead.'

CHAPTER TWO

A FULL minute went by, and a full minute in a dark car in a fast darkling world can be a very long time.

The man ... Magnus David, he had told her ... had his

16

attention on the track, and it was a very treacherous track. Even in daylight its necessary detours round rock outcrops, fallen logs and encroaching trees would have been a hazard, but now it was a demanding, full-time job. Yet Paddy was not thinking of the difficulties the man was dealing with, she was thinking only of Jerry, that nice idiot, that mate, that Magnus to Maryrose.

'He called himself Magnus,' she heard herself saying dully. It could not be true, that fellow witness to last year's September and last year's spring could not be gone. She could never think of that eternal elf, that constant sprite, as——

'And you called yourself Maryrose,' he said coldly.

'Only out of fun.'

'But I don't think poor Jeremy's part was in fun.' A pause. 'No, *I* am Magnus.'

'Yes, you said so.'

'Well?'

'Well what?' she asked.

'Doesn't that explain things?'

'How do you mean?'

'I was senior to Jeremy, I was bigger, stronger, more successful, more experienced, a man of the world, it was only natural that Jeremy——'

'Yes?'

'That he emulated me.'

Only natural! That his brother emulated him! What kind of person was this?

'So,' concluded Magnus David, 'in your game of make-believe Jeremy was me.'

'You're quite wrong,' Paddy corrected him coolly. 'There was no game of makebelieve.'

'Maryrose? Magnus?'

'That was only a joke.'

'And the rest—was it a joke, too?'

'What rest?'

'One year, twelve months, fifty-two weeks of remembering. Was that a joke, Miss Travis?'

'No, not a joke, just a reminder by Jerry of a good month.'

'Yet no reminder from you,' he pointed out.

'Oh, you're wrong,' she protested. 'I remembered.'

'Please go on.'

'And it was a very good month.'

'Just that? Just good?'

'I said very good,' Paddy repeated.

'Yet it only lasted that long for you? A month?'

'What do you mean?'

'We'll come to that later.' He braked for a fat wombat who decided at that moment to cross the track. 'No wonder they get killed,' he said absently.

'No, not later, now.' Paddy was not watching the wombat, she was too concerned with herself. She did not know what was coming from this man, she only knew that it would be unpleasant, but she was still not going to be set aside like that.

'Very well then,' he conceded promptly, 'was it just for a month or——'

'What do you mean by "it"?' Paddy broke in.

'Whatever was staged there.'

'Nothing was staged there. I presume you're meaning Pelican Beach?'

'I am. Was it just for a month or——'

'Or?' she questioned.

'Until now. Until this.'

'I don't understand you, Mr David.'

'All this,' he repeated harshly, 'all part of the David
... and Jeremy was a David ... estate.'

'I still don't understand you.'

'But I understand you,' he said harshly.

'You can't. I—I mean, there's nothing to be understood.'

'Oh, come off it! I'm not one of your tender wards,
house-mother, I'm an adult. Well adult. I'm thirty-five,
more than twice Jeremy's age when he fell for your sly
trap.'

About to object angrily at that 'sly trap', Paddy stared
at him instead, stared incredulously.

'You couldn't be!'

'Thirty-five? Thank you, madam, it's nice to be told,
even falsely, that you don't look your age.'

'Jerry didn't look twenty.' Paddy was saying it to herself, not him. 'But he couldn't have been, he wasn't——'

'Only seventeen rising eighteen?'

'Yes.'

'He was, though, Miss Travis.'

'But I was twenty.' Paddy almost whispered it in her
dismay.

'And Jeremy was under eighteen,' Magnus David repeated.

'He didn't say so.'

'Did you ask?'

'We never talked about things like that, only
about——'

'Yes?'

But Paddy found she could not go on.

Magnus David waited a while, then changed to the
subject of wards.

'I have to break it to you that they're not tender ones,

as I just said, they're the usual horrors.' A thin smile. 'I thought you would like to know.'

'I'll cope,' she assured him.

'I doubt it.' A shrug. 'Their particular category' ... *particular* category? ... 'needs years of experience, something you haven't got. However, I was well aware of that when I chose you from the applicants.'

'How did you choose me?' Paddy asked. 'And how did you know where to go to choose?'

'I think you mean how did I track you down? How did I find out that you were connected with Jeremy?'

'I was never "connected", as you put it, with Jerry.'

He ignored that.

'I chose you, Miss Travis, because I'd previously found out about you, and it was too good a chance to miss.'

'A chance not to be missed?'

'I said that.'

She was silent a while, then at last she found words.

'You took me on even though I was inexperienced ... well, inexperienced in situations if not in theory, simply because it was to good a chance to miss?'

'Yes.'

'You didn't think "Poor wards"?'

'I did, but I put the thought aside.'

'Why?'

'Because I wanted to see you, estimate you, observe you ... weigh you up.'

'Weigh me up?' she echoed.

'Yes.'

'For what?'

'You could say' ... thinly and with a thin twist to his lips ... 'to be found wanting.'

'Yes, and I think you would want that.'

'Perhaps I did.'

'No perhaps,' refused Paddy wretchedly. How could she feel less than wretched with such a wretched man? She bit hard on her lip.

'Yet you were quoted to me as a great benefactor,' she said angrily.

'I am. Believe me, I'm a very charitable man. I inherited a considerable estate from my uncle, and the business it deals with is expanding every day.'

'Bananas.'

'Bananas?' He glanced quickly at her.

'It said so on the map in your Sydney office,' she explained.

'Bananas on the coast, yes, but we've left the coast. In case you haven't noticed we're climbing.'

'Then what is the inherited business?' asked Paddy.

His look was sharp this time. 'Yoothamurra?' he prompted.

'I don't know what it means.'

'It's aboriginal for great luck.'

'Well?'

'Well, don't try to pretend you're unaware.'

'I am unaware,' she insisted.

Magnus David gave an unpleasant, disbelieving laugh, then he resumed again.

'I set aside a large portion of my—well, fortune, you could call it—for the association *you* work for, Miss Travis.'

'Only out of goodheartedness, of course.' Paddy's lips were curled.

'Of course. What else?'

'I think a great deal else, Mr David.'

'You're right,' he agreed blandly. 'As a matter of interest, you come in as well.'

'I?'

'You.'

'But——'

'I had, through devious methods, discovered who you were and where you worked. So instead of donating to one of the usual charities that I might have, I chose the Closer Families Association. Your concern.'

'That's true.'

'Because,' he continued, and even in the dark that had descended now Paddy could see the man's derision, 'you were involved.'

'That's true. I work for Closer Families.'

'That was not the involvement I meant, but it will do just now. You worked for Closer Families and now' ... a deliberate pause ... 'you work for me.'

'I think,' said Paddy jerkily, her mind made up before he explained any more, 'that can be rectified.'

'I don't think,' he said smoothly back, 'that it can.'

'I don't understand you.'

'You said that before.'

'Will you tell me, please?' she asked.

'Gladly. Briefly. Yesterday you signed a paper.'

'That is so,' Paddy agreed.

'Then it's a pity you didn't read it, Miss Travis, because—it's binding.'

'Binding?'

'You are bound, under a penalty of cash repayment, to work for me.'

'But I have no money,' Paddy pointed out.

'That was another thing,' he said, still smoothly, 'that I took the precaution of ascertaining.'

'My lack of money?'

'Yes.'

'You've been very painstaking,' she said coldly.

'I always am.'

'I—I can't follow you. I can't credit what you're saying. Why do you dislike me so much?'

'Have I said so?'

'You've acted so.'

'By choosing you out of a score of applicants for the job? Is that dislike?'

'In this case, yes. How did you do it?'

'Find you?'

'Yes.'

'It was both simple yet time-consuming. The pertinent Personal and Missing Friends ad, I'd noted . . . incidentally Jeremy died only recently, hence this year's insertion . . . quoted "Remember September." I checked back. There was only one September Jeremy had not been at home. That was the September following his three months in bed, when the doctor suggested a little toughening up by himself down at the beach. Last year, to be more precise.'

'Three months in bed?' Paddy gasped.

He nodded. 'Jeremy spent a lot of time in bed. He only went to school briefly.'

. . . *'I've never had a friend. I didn't have enough time at school to collect one. I was considered delicate, ho-ho, so I had lessons at home.'* Jerry's dear boyish voice.

'So I remembered Jeremy going down to the beach,' Magnus David continued.

'Your beach, I think.' It was all coming back now—the caretaker, the deference he always had given to Jerry.

'Yes.'

'So you checked?' Paddy prompted. 'Had you always checked on Jerry like that?'

'The answer is Yes.' A pause. 'You do with Jeremys.'

'What do you mean?'

'You must know.'

'I don't,' she insisted.

'Prognosis nil. That's a medical term, Miss Travis, for no future. For a short thread in the tapestry of life. But of course you must have known that.'

'How? Why? What are you saying?'

For answer he gave a brief laugh.

'Jeremy had no time left,' he went on, 'he never had had time. It was a miracle he reached the years that he did.'

'Please go on,' she said quietly.

'So I checked which September, and the rest was easy. Jeremy might not have bothered to find out your name, but Walsh knew.'

'The caretaker?'

'Yes.'

'Letters,' Paddy nodded. She said it dully.

'Letters,' Magnus David agreed.

'But I still don't understand. What did it matter? Was Jerry asking for me?'

'Oh, no, nothing like that. Don't go all sentimental too late. Also don't go too fast. That will come later.'

'Then?'

'I found out your name ... something which Jeremy hadn't, and it would have made it awkward in law had the thing gone through.'

'The—thing?'

His lips tightened. 'I found out your name,' he resumed, 'after which running you to earth was comparatively simple. I found out where you worked. Are you catching on now?'

'No.'

'Not very alert today, are you, Maryrose?' He smiled without amusement.

'What—what else?'

'What you already know.' A shrug. 'I decided on your line of business, the business of orphans.'

'Destitutes, too,' Paddy came in woodenly, and he nodded.

'It seemed as good a charity as any to me, especially with a house too large for one. So——'

'So?'

'I contacted your Mr Aston ... it is Aston?'

'Yes, Aston. Then?'

'Can't you guess?'

'No, Mr David, I can't guess,' she snapped. 'And don't try to concoct a significant interlude between Jerry and me, because there wasn't any.'

'No? But there must have been something.'

Paddy looked at the man through the darkness, for night definitely had fallen now.

'What?' she challenged.

'You tell me and I'll tell you.' He laughed scornfully. 'But to prompt you I'll tell you part of it.'

'Part?'

'There are two parts, happily, then unhappily, for you.'

'Yes?'

'Part One : Poor Jeremy left you everything he possessed, Miss Travis. That's your happy part.'

'I'm touched, but they would be nothing—not, as you tell me, at the age of eighteen.'

'He was only seventeen then. You see, he wrote the thing at once. *Seventeen*, not even the lower legal age that is now currently accepted. Well, are you starting to catch on now?'

'Catch on?' she asked.

'He left a will at seventeen, a very emotional and affectionate piece of prose, but' ... a pause ... 'he was seventeen nonetheless, and that's your Part Two, the unhappy part.'

'Did—did Jerry know his future?'

'His lack of it, you mean? Yes.'

'I said once he looked young and he didn't like it.' Paddy caught her lip with her teeth and held back a sob.

'Oh, he was intelligent,' Magnus shrugged. 'Don't think because he made a will as a minor he was unaware of things. Not Jeremy. No, he would be depending on me.'

'On you?'

'To see it through.'

'Which you won't.'

'Which I won't.—Tell me, Miss Travis, as a matter of interest, what did you do to mesmerise him?'

'Mesmerise?' she queried.

'I said that.'

'I did nothing,' Paddy insisted.

'Which is what you will be receiving.'

'And would have, anyway, for Jerry had nothing.'

'Oh, no, my dear, you're wrong.'

'But I tell you, he was as hard-up as I was.'

... *Race you to the buoy. Last out of the water buys the lunch* ...

'He had nothing *then*.' Magnus must have read her thoughts. He negotiated a sharp bend. 'But a year has

26

passed. An estate has been wound up. Are you catching on at last?'

'No.'

'Then Mr Aston was wrong when he said you had high intelligence. I'd label you dumb.'

'Please tell me—and you can leave out Mr Aston.'

He shrugged. 'Very well then. You've been bequeathed ... or would have been under different circumstances ... a very comfortable sum. In short—a fortune.'

'From Jerry?'

'From Jeremy. But' ... and the man beside Paddy paused significantly ... 'only, at that irresponsible age, if *I* say so. Ordinarily I would say so, and readily. I have more than enough money of my own. But I'm not satisfied, Miss Travis, and that's why I've brought you up here. I want to know why Jeremy did it, also how I'm to react.'

'You?' she queried.

'I was his mentor, teacher, authoritarian, guardian, adviser. You have to be to an afterthought brother who arrives when you yourself are almost a man. Because Jeremy was immature, and because I was responsible for him, I am now in the position of judge. Well, have we got that straight in the end?'

'You might have,' said Paddy coldly. 'I haven't.'

'No?'

'No. Also I don't intend to try. So just turn back to the station, Mr David.'

'You mean the conditional stop? Turnabout Creek? But there's no train either way before tomorrow morning, and even then only if you ring the nearest station for them to alert the guard, and there's no phone until we reach the house.'

'I'm resigning,' she snapped.

'Before you even start!'

'Yes. I couldn't work for a man like you.'

'I gathered in a calling like this that you worked for the ideal, not the employer.'

'Sometimes the employer makes that impossible. You would.'

'All very well, but aren't you forgetting the agreement you signed?'

'No, I'm not forgetting, but what else, apart from my having to borrow from someone to repay you for my ticket and anything else you have put out, could my resignation mean to me?'

'It could cancel any future assignments through the C.F.A.'

She had not thought of that, had not thought that anyone would be so mean as to think of it either, but a glance at the man beside her told her that he would ... and had.

'Then I'll scrub floors. Or wash dishes. Or——'

'Or marry? That's another idea for you now that your previous one has gone sour. Tell me' ... before she could break in ... 'how did you find out Jeremy's potential?'

'Potential?' she queried.

'What he could one day mean in the almighty dollar?'

'I hate you! You're the worst man I could even dream up in a ghastly nightmare.—But tell *me* something for a change. Why do you despise me this much?'

'Because,' said Magnus David, reaching the top of the mountain at last and turning into a drive that seemed suddenly to have opened up from nowhere, 'I loved him.'

'Loved him?'

'Loved my brother Jeremy.' He halted the big black car at a big white edifice. 'I loved him very much.'

He leaned across her and opened her door.

'Madam, we've arrived.'

CHAPTER THREE

IT was not a house, it was a castle—that was Paddy's first impression. Almost she turned to the man now obviously awaiting her reaction to fling at him:

'It's a castle, and you are its king.'

She might as well have said it. Just as he had read her before, Magnus David read her again.

'No, not the king, merely the owner. There are a number of such castles dotted around the north coast, built either by exiled remittance lords or ambitious one-time stablehands who made good in their new country and proved it in the best manner they could think. A fine house.'

'Castle,' she corrected.

'Castle, castelo, palace, palacio, call it what you will so long as it's home. But I forgot, it's not to be that to you.'

'You mean I can go after all?' she asked eagerly.

'No, I meant you would never allow it to be your home.'

'With you in it? No,' she agreed definitely. After a pause she asked: 'And what were your forefathers, lords or stablehands?'

'This forefather was a fore-uncle. I—*we*' ... he looked

at her cruelly, remindingly ... 'inherited from him. He was a——'

'A banana baron?' Paddy broke in before he could finish. She had heard of the banana barons of the north coast. She added with deliberate impertinence: 'Do I bow?'

He let that pass. He helped her out of the car, then led the way up the steep, imposing flight of curved stairs to a wide patio. On every rise there was a tub of oleander. There was an immense front door ... portal, Paddy found herself thinking of it ... and it was flung open to display a long, red-carpeted hall.

'*Not* put down for you,' Magnus David assured her, 'so please don't feel embarrassed. No, it's been in use for years. As long, possibly, as the house, which is so old by colonial standards, and so significant of its period, that there's been an approach from the National Trust.'

'I wasn't feeling embarrassed,' Paddy replied, 'I was feeling a little dubious about such a beautiful carpet and four wards.'

'Oh, they don't live this side.'

'Yet I do?' Paddy turned to him in righteous protest.

He smiled almost pityingly back at her. 'The last thing I would want to do ... with you ... is flaunt convention. Oh, no, I'm just being polite and having you here first.'

'To show me around?'

'And give you a general idea of the place, of the kind of job it is.'

'Oh, I know *that*. I'm *trained*, Mr David.'

'But not experienced, I hear. I've no doubt that lacking an aircraft to practise on a man could still be taught to fly on paper, but I can tell you I wouldn't be a passenger when he did reach the controls.'

'Meaning?'

'Meaning how will you manage four actually in your hands instead of at the end of a pen?'

'Well, you won't be one of my "passengers", will you?' she answered smartly. 'I anticipate little trouble. Unlike you, Mr David, they will be the needing ones, the unfortunate, the unbelonging ones—something you never were.'

'You were yourself?'

'No, but I've been trained——'

'Trained!' The laugh was more a sneer. 'All the same, you're quite wrong. I ... and my brother ... were orphans.'

'But privileged ones.'

'Can an orphan be privileged?' he came back.

He let a moment go by, then said: 'My father died when I was sixteen. It was a big blow. We were very close. But the blow was minimized with the amazing news of my mother's pregnancy. She had been married at a very young age, had had me, then that was that.' He shrugged and extended his hands. They were big, working hands, Paddy noted, not delicate like Jerry's had been. Yet there was something else about them ... a kind of gentleness for all their firmness, as though he sometimes dealt with gentle situations.—But gentleness in this man?

'Jeremy was a complete surprise,' he was saying, 'and a lovely surprise ... at least it would have been if she had lived.'

'Your mother died, too?'

'One year after my father and following Jeremy's birth. I hated Jeremy for a while for that. Then I came to my senses and I—well, I loved him instead. Loved him much more, I think.'

It was all making sense now. This man had gone from one extreme to the other, from resentment to devotion. Paddy could see how he had disliked her so much . . . and yet, she thought, if he had loved Jerry, *really* loved him, shouldn't he have been pleased that for a while, anyway, his brother had been glad? 'Maryrose: Remember September? Magnus.' Shouldn't he have smiled, not scowled over that?

'My aunt Mirabel brought Jeremy up while I finished my education,' Magnus David went on.

'Jerry grew up here?'

'I did, too, once away from school. Aunt and Uncle had no children and it was a well-known fact that the property would be ours one day.' There was the slightest emphasis on 'well-known', and Paddy flinched.

'Is there all that much money in bananas, Baron David?' she asked boldly.

'We've left the coast,' he reminded her impatiently. 'I told you so on the way up. We're now on a plateau.'

'But there are bananas.' Her glance had fallen on a huge platter of them on the hall table.

'From the valley plantation,' he shrugged.

'You have that as well?'

'Yes.'

'As well as—what?'

'But you already know. You must know.'

'I don't—I said so before.'

'Too busy on other things down at the beach,' he said thinly. Before she could speak, he told her: 'Yoothamurra, meaning Great Luck.'

'Also meaning——?'

'Meaning our—my stud.'

'A stud. Yoothamurra Stud.' Yes, yes, she *had* heard of

it, and it all came back. It was a very big, very successful breeding and training complex. It had a long string of big racing firsts, an enviable breeding record. She had forgotten, but now she recalled. Yoothamurra ... Great Luck.

'Horses,' she half-mumbled.

'Blood stuff,' he told her.

'Rewarding?' She made a question of it.

He gave a dry laugh. 'Croesus would have been well satisfied.' A pause. 'Now are you satisfied, Miss Travis? Is your curiosity—so-called—duly assuaged?' Not giving her time to answer, he said : 'If so, I'll proceed to show you around.' He strode down the hall, snapping on lights as he went, and perforce Paddy followed.

'I'd keep it lit,' he explained over his shoulder, 'but we depend on our own plant here, so have to curb ourselves.' He opened a door and nodded for Paddy to look in.

The rooms were all large and expensively furnished but shabby from age as well now, and Paddy reluctantly praised this to herself, for she had always loved good things grown old.

She was careful not to let him see her approval, though, as she peered round the many doors he flung open.

'It's very big,' she said at last.

'This is only half of it. My half. The other is identical, though not' ... he grinned ... 'identically furnished.'

'I should think not. Heirlooms would be unwise for children.'

'... Scarcely children.'

She looked quickly at him at that; she had imagined the usual age groups in this group of four. Say—five to ten, or six to twelve, or—Nothing younger than four, since Closer Families made it a rule that little ones were

33

never boarded out while they were still in the nursery stage, and nothing older than sixteen, though sixteen-year-olds, of course, did occur when fifteen-year-olds had another birthday.

'How many boys?' she asked.

'Four.'

'How many gi——' Paddy stopped. 'But—but you said, your secretary said there were only four altogether.'

'There are only four.'

'All boys?'

'All boys. Anything wrong in that?'

'No, nothing wrong, but it's considered ... I mean, the C.F.A. considers a mixed family as much better.'

'They will be mixed ... with you.'

Paddy did not comment on that.

He was watching her narrowly.

'I rather thought,' he drawled, 'you would relish the idea of being the sole female.'

'I'm a house-mother. I accept what comes my way. But no doubt you're pleased.'

'Of course, but then I requested it that way.'

'You requested all boys?'

'Yes.'

'But Closer Families allots, it doesn't concede to requests.'

'Like to bet on it?' He was lighting a cigarette. In spite of the fact that he was as much a city man as a country ... he had that Sydney office ... he did it in the old bush manner. He rolled and moulded the cigarette himself. Paddy watched him fascinated, listening to the dry whisper of the flattened tobacco, the rumple of the paper. It was only when he was licking the edges together that she became aware that he was watching her watching him.

She flushed and half-turned away.

'Yes, four boys,' he resumed. 'Like to guess their ages?'

'Six, eight, ten, twelve, maybe thirteen. I know they're all loners.'

'That's right, they're loners, but you're wrong with the ages.'

'Then five, seven, nine, eleven.'

'You're too far down, too junior. They're not such tender grapes, or should I say in these parts not such tender bananas.'

Paddy said, 'I would sooner you tell me their ages.'

'Begin at fourteen,' he suggested.

She stared at him in disbelief, but somewhere in the disbelief the memory of this man saying on the trip up that the intake was of a 'particular category.'—*Particular* category?

'You can't be serious,' she said aloud.

'Fourteen, fifteen, sixteen and rising seventeen.'

'I don't believe you.'

'Then you'd better begin.'

'The Board wouldn't allow it.'

'Like to bet on it?' he said again.

There was a silence for a few moments.

'You must have made a *very* large donation,' Paddy observed coldly.

'I did.'

There was silence, then Paddy said, even more coldly : 'But I can see why.'

'House-mother?'

'Cheap labour,' she flung at him, 'for your stud.'

'You could add the plantation,' he suggested amicably, 'I can do with labour there as well. But as regards the stud, don't forget girls work in studs, too, in fact in all my friends' studs they're more sought-after than boys. They have a touch.' He exhaled. 'Have you a touch?'

'Only a touch of disgust at your sly method of assuring yourself of future help. Hands these days are very hard to get, I'm told.'

'They are, indeed. I recently lost one very outstanding trainer,' Magnus frowned.

'But you won't be in such a position again, will you? Not if you play your cards right. Surely you'll score one out of four.'

'Horses are an affinity,' he said shortly, 'rapport is not a thing that can be ordered or arranged.'

'And he had this gift, this ex-trainer of yours?'

There was a pause. Then:

'He got results.'

'Which you should continue to get surely with one out of four. Oh, yes, four boys was a very good idea.'

In answer he turned away from her, turned quite violently, and walked to the other end of the room. He stood there.

'Damn you,' he said at last.

'What do you mean, Mr David?'

'You know it's not that, you know it's—Jeremy.'

She went to retort, then stopped. 'You mean,' she deciphered quietly, 'four Jeremys, one at fourteen, one at fifteen, one at sixteen, and one rising seventeen?'

'Yes.'

'But Jerry was their age too once.'

'But he was ill, he was not as they are, he was not as he should have been. He missed that, and I missed it. He can't have it ever, but I can, and I will. Oh, I know you don't understand, but——' His voice broke off, but when he came back to Paddy from the end of the room again he was composed once more.

'Your next question,' he prompted, 'will be why I got myself a house-mother when at those ages obviously a housekeeper would have done. But with Closer Families it was obligatory, and it had to be Closer Families—because of you.'

'So you could assess me,' she nodded. 'Find me wanting.'

'Yes.'

'You particularly requested me.'

'Yes.'

'And I, flattered, a willing victim, fell for the trap.'

'Well, it had to happen some time,' he said, 'you falling for a trap, I mean. How many traps have you set yourself? *One*, at least I know.'

Paddy ignored that. It was hard, but she made herself do it. Arguing would get nowhere with this man.

'Mr David, is there anything else?' she inquired.

'Most certainly. Your room.'

'That will be over there.' Paddy pointed to the opposed side of the house.

'Oh, no.'

'But you said so. You said it wasn't here. You said perish the thought.'

'I also did not say you were to live over there.' He gestured to where she had.

'But——'

'If it were daylight I would take you out and show you the architecture of this house.'

'Castle,' she corrected frostily.

'Well, it could be, for like most castles it comprises another inner wing. Your wing.'

'Mine?' she echoed. 'But a house-mother lives *with* her wards. Not literally exactly, but——'

'I should hope not, not with this advanced quartet.'

'But still' ... still ignoring him ... 'as near to them as next door.'

'Which you shall be. Your small wing is actually dovetailed between this side and that. You will be as next door to them as you will be to me.' He smiled blandly.

'But it isn't done like that,' Paddy fretted.

'How would you know, you've never performed resident duties before.'

'The personal, the intimate touch would be lost, Mr David.'

'With them—or with me?'

'You know what I mean.'

'Then with four boys in their teens, one of them in his later teens, that is what I want, must have. I also think, because of your history, you should want it as well.'

'There was no history,' she said heatedly.

He merely shrugged.

'Anyway, it's all very irregular,' she persisted, 'everything about this assignment is irregular. The same sex throughout, the advanced ages, the——'

'The——?' he prompted.

'The—the reason you've worked it out like this.'

'I didn't work it out, your principal did, after he heard my request.'

'You mean after you put a large cheque in his hand.'

He did not comment on that, instead he demanded:

'Finish what you started to say, tell me the reason why I worked it out like this.'

Paddy was beyond tactfulness and discretion now. She turned wildly on the man.

'The reason, as you've already said, was Jerry. You feel you've been deprived of him at their ages, so you have brought them here to try to win back your lost years. Also you've brought me, to find out and to preserve any little thing I'd learned about Jerry but you had not.'

A few moments went by in utter silence. Somewhere in the big house a clock chimed and Paddy could feel each beat as though it was her heart. She dared not look at the man, but she could sense his deep rage ... and somewhere deeper, but she refused to acknowledge it, his deeper pain.

'You disapprove of love, then?' he asked at last.

'No, but I don't like your brand—possessive, enclosing, depriving everyone else.'

'I'd hardly call you deprived. Your suite, you will find, is quite lavish.'

'Not that,' she almost shouted at him, 'but Jerry as I knew him, that other witness to September. You're only seeing Jerry's passing as your deprivation, never your brother's.' A pause. 'Never mine.'

'So there was something,' he said coldly.

'There was spring—something I believe you never had, Mr David. I think spring passed you by. And now, if you don't mind, I'm tired, I'd like to——'

'Gladly,' he said thickly, and he advanced on her. Before Paddy could reply to him, could evade him, he pushed her to a door she had not noticed before. He opened it, almost threw in her bags, then almost threw in her.

'You'll find it self-contained,' he said frigidly. 'A woman comes in, so no need to think about breakfast or any other meals. You're the "mother" only, not the housekeeper. There'll be food in the refrigerator if you're hungry. If you need anything, tap on the door, but don't tap on the other door, the boys' door. Their quarters are empty, they're spending the night out at the stud.'

'Isn't that rather rash of you?' Paddy shot at him.

'No, they like sleeping at the stables.'

'I meant—the other.'

'What, Miss Travis?'

'I meant if it was questionable of me with Jerry on an empty beach, couldn't it be more questionable still with Jerry's brother in an empty house—? Questionable for *you*, too. No one else in the house. A woman as close as next door.—No, don't answer. I know the reply already. Perish the thought.'

'You have it exactly. Goodnight, Miss Travis.' He closed the door and Paddy turned the key.

After she had done so, she came blindly into the room, found a chair and sank down.

And cried.

CHAPTER FOUR

PADDY cried ... and cried.

She cried for Jerry. She cried because she was tired and discouraged. She cried because she had believed she had won this job on her merits, but as it had turned out the position had only been given to her because of Magnus David's cheque. She cried because she was about to be tried and found wanting, and how could she not be found that when she *was* wanting, wanting very desperately at this moment for ordinary friendship, ordinary goodwill, ordinary kindness. He had given her nothing like that.

What was it he had said? she wept into her handkerchief. It had been something about her not being deprived, not with a suite like he was providing her. As though that could count, as though creature comfort mattered, but all the same Paddy emerged from the handkerchief and looked around.

Not knowing what to expect, she regarded her wing between two wings ... then gave a gasp. Why, it was quite beautiful, she saw. The same lovely old furniture adorned it, the same soft colours enhanced it, as the master unit. They might not be provided for the wards, but they had been for her.

She wondered what the windows looked out on. Just now they held only darkness and stars, but at daytime the view should be stunning, for he, Magnus David, had told her they were on a plateau, and a plateau would naturally command the countryside for miles.

The dovetailed flat consisted of a bed-sitting room, bathroom and small kitchen with eating recess should the occupier wish to dine alone. That would not happen, Paddy resolved, for she was a firm believer in a family sitting round a table (in this instance no male head, of course) though tonight she would have to eat alone ... and yes, she was getting hungry. The last time she had eaten had been on the train, and well down the coast. I'm sorry, Jerry, she said aloud, but you always did tell me I was hollow inside. She laughed a little at that and felt a great deal better. She knew Jerry would have liked that reminder.

She opened a small fridge and found a chicken salad laid out. A cupboard nearby produced crisp rolls. She put both on a tray and took the meal to the window, and there she sat and ate. There was a little breeze turning the leaves of a tree outside. It was rather a warm breeze, for these were the hotter latitudes, but there was a crispness somewhere, and that would be because this was a mountain top ... many mountains but one top. It would make for crispness. The meal finished, Paddy leaned right out of the window and took a deep breath. It was quite exhilarating; no wonder bloodstock prospered here.

Not quite in keeping with plateau air and horses, though, was the large dish of bananas on the bench— apples seemed more in keeping with horses; but Paddy was to learn afterwards that with so many banana plantations literally at their feet, and one of them belonging to the stud, bananas were always there for the taking. She took one now, peeled it in the four ribbons that bananas should be peeled, and looked around her again.

That door through which she had come ... no, been pushed ... was his. She saw there was a corresponding door almost opposite, apparently belonging to the boys' side, and she went curiously across. They were not there, he had said, but there was nothing to stop her looking around. She saw a key hanging on a hook, and applied it. The key turned and she entered the wards' domain.

It was a much larger unit than her own, nearer the size, she decided, of the main section, his section. But even with bedrooms to spare the boys had still evidently elected to sleep in one room, and Paddy smiled gently at that. How they clung together, these unbelonging ones; they would quibble, actively fight on many occasions, but they all shared that deep-down bond, that fellow need. Poor little ones, she thought tenderly, then clapped her hand to her mouth. She was dealing with four teenagers, not juniors, and Magnus David was waiting to see how she would do it. What he had done himself, Paddy saw ungraciously, was quite faultless. The room was cheerful yet not consciously so. It was bright and casual. It was home. It seemed she had something to keep up with, she grimaced.

She left the room ... more a dormitory with its four beds covered in tartan weave ... and looked in at the quite huge kitchen. Good, she liked a huge kitchen, particularly since she was a firm believer in families, children families, eating in the kitchen. Not only did it make it easier for that extra slice of toast, the need for which invariably cropped up, but it bound the eaters closer together in some homely way. She was pleased to see that the housekeeper evidently shared the same views, for there were several signs of the last meal still present ... an unrolled napkin, a crumb on the floor, a salt shaker still sitting in the middle of the long scrubbed table.

She looked into the other room, the hobby or recreation room, she guessed, expecting a record player, the customary games, bits of wire and pliers as someone tried their hand on a crystal set, the usual things teenage boys like to do, but she found very little. However, she did find horses. Pictures of horses on the wall, books about horses on the table, ribbons, several trophies and actually a saddle that one of them must be mending.

Oh, yes, Mr Magnus David, she said aloud, you've done yourself very well indeed. You can't possibly lose here.

There was nothing else to look at, so Paddy went back to her tucked-in unit and decided to run a bath.

She took her time in the tub. She was tired, but she felt sure she would not sleep tonight, so she delayed going to bed for as long as she could. Though it was past twelve when at last she did make a move, the lights in the master flat were still on, she could see them when she leaned out of the window for a last breath of wonderful air. So he was not sleeping yet either.

Paddy put her own light out, got into a very comfortable bed, prepared for hours of introspection ... and slept at once.

She was awakened by a noise that sounded like a marching army. It was daylight, and the morning sun was buttering the windowsill, yet barely so. It must be very early, judged Paddy of the meagre yellow, and she cuddled gratefuly back into the rugs again.

But a second noise prevented her from slipping off, and she resentfully opened her eyes to see what was happening. She could discover nothing, then, about to dismiss it as imagination, she saw—an eye. She must be dreaming things. Solitary eyes do not suddenly appear in a crack of a blind unless there is something behind them. Paddy got out of her bed and approached the eye.

It was blue and young, one could always tell the eyes of the young, for they were extra clear. But how ... and why ... and what if the eye, and what went with the eye, fell? The house was elevated, its ground floor given over to garages, so any fall would be most distressing.

Paddy pulled up the blind. It was the slatted type and that was why she had been able to see the eye and the eye see her. She heard a noise as though something or someone was trying to retreat in a hurry, then another noise as a ladder, or a plank, fell.

She looked down on the horrified face of a smallish boy and was horrified herself. Evidently he had crawled across to the window from the next-door window on a rigged plank, and the rigging had loosened and the plank had fallen to the ground. That would be the noise she had just heard.

'Help me,' said the boy, and, deciding it was no time to deliver a lecture, not with such a drop to the ground, Paddy complied. He must be the youngest ward, she thought gratefully, grateful because anything more than his height and weight would have been beyond her strength. She supported him until he got a footing, then helped him haul himself into her room. There he stood apprehensively awaiting her censure.

'Well?' asked Paddy sternly.

'I'm sorry.' A pause. 'Don't tell him.'

'Him?'

'The boss. Mr David.'

'You deserve to be reported,' said Paddy, still sternly. 'However, if he's as bad as that, then no, I won't. I'll deal with you myself.'

'He's not bad, he's a decent bloke, and that's why I don't want him to know. I'm sorry I came, but it had to be me—the others said so.'

'Yes, they do that to the youngest, so you must learn ... what's your name?'

'Paul.'

'You must learn, Paul, to stand up for yourself.'

'But when I do, even if I stretch, I'm not as tall as they are.'

'Not to worry,' she assured him, 'you'll catch up.'

'I won't, though, I'm the second eldest but still the smallest. I used to mind once, but I like it now, because I'll be the jockey, you see.'

'Yes, I see,' said Paddy drily. 'And what about the rest?'

'Strappers, stablehands, all with a view to being the

trainer, but I won't have to worry about that.' Paul smiled triumphantly, and it was such a wide smile for a small person that Paddy dropped the lecture she had decided would be appropriate, a lecture driving home to Paul that there should be more to life than racing. Anyway, what would have been the use? Obviously the boy was horse-besotted, obviously ... remembering the saddle in the recreation room last night ... they all were.

'All right,' she said, 'I'm not telling, but you'll have to tell me why you're here.'

'We were anxious to find out what you were like.'

'Fat? Thin? Tall? Short? Dark? Fair? Old? Young?'

'No,' said Paul. 'What you were *like*.'

Paddy understood. She had seen too many quick, eager, intuitive child looks *not* to understand.

'Well?' she asked.

'I reckon you're all right.'

'Thank you, Paul. If you go back to your quarters now I'll join you very soon. Did you have breakfast out at the stables?'

'Yes, but Mr David doesn't bar you from having two, and it's pretty good grub. You'll see.'

'Who cooks it?' she asked.

'Mrs Dermott. She wants to see you, too.'

'But I don't think she was in this plank stunt.'

'No, she hadn't arrived. She has now, I can smell toast.'

Paddy could, too, and she turned to shower and dress.

'What will I tell them your name is?' Paul asked.

Paddy hesitated. In her day sessions she had been Aunt, but the children had been young children. Paddy, she toyed. No, not quite.

'Miss Paddy,' she told Paul. Well, she could scarcely say 'Miss Padua'.

46

'Out!' she ordered, and unlocked the intervening door, put Paul on the other side, then quickly bathed and got into her clothes.

The boys were round the table when she went in, but, well trained earlier by Closer Families, or perhaps more recently by Mr David, they all got up.

'Good morning, boys.'

'Good morning, Miss Paddy.'

The housekeeper, who had been stacking tins in a walk-in pantry, came out and beamed at Paddy.

'I'm Mrs Dermott, my dear. It's good to have a woman around the place. I do the cleaning and cooking ... did Mr David tell you? ... you look after the boys. Boys, exchange names.'

'She's Paddy. She said so.'

'Miss Paddy,' corected Paddy. She looked at the tallest and obviously eldest boy. 'You would be———?'

'Richard. He's Mark. That's John. And you've just met Paul.'

'Paul, the future jockey.'

'So he hopes.'

'And who hopes to be trainer?'

This started a babble, it seemed they all wanted to be a trainer, or stud manager, or something equally exalted.

'But,' said senior Richard, 'you have to start at the bottom. Sweeping and cleaning and feeding and all that.'

'Yes, all that,' they cheerfully accepted.

... Oh, yes, Mr David, Paddy said silently, your future supply of hands *is* assured. She sat down at the table and Mrs Dermott brought a huge plate.

'I can't eat all that!' protested Paddy.

'You have to,' she was assured on all sides.

About to correct them, tell them that they might have

47

to but that she didn't, Paddy found the smell of the bacon quite irresistible, and fell to with an appetite that surprised her.

Mrs Dermott meanwhile was busy packing lunches.

'These two are for the two youngest,' she informed Paddy, 'they go to the valley school. Mark, John, you better get down to the gate to catch the school bus.'

'And what about you two?' Paddy asked the senior boys. 'You can't be finished with school at your age.'

'We study at night, and Mr David said you'll be helping us there.'

'I will, but——'

'There's no secondary classes in the valley school, and anyway, Mr David got permission to let us work in the stud because that's what we want.'

'And what he wants, no doubt.' But Paddy kept that to herself.

The older boys were rushing ahead with their meals the same as the younger, then also receiving a packed lunch.

'We're going out on an exercise with Mr David today,' they explained. 'If we're spending the time at the stables, we get grub there.'

'Yes,' said Paddy a little faintly, wondering when she would see them again, wondering why she was needed here. But before she could do any asking, they had taken up their lunches and left with a cheery Hooroo.

'Bright bunch, aren't they?' smiled Mrs Dermott. 'It's because they're so happy. They're square pegs in square holes ... is that right? ... but then it's a boys' world here.'

'But one boy didn't make it.' Rightly or wrongly, and Paddy knew it was wrongly, Paddy was going to probe, probe Mrs Dermott.

'Yes, him, poor dear lad,' Mrs Dermott nodded.

'Yes ... Jerry.'

'Did you know him, then, Miss Paddy?'

'Just Paddy. Yes, a little.'

'It was terribly sad, but then, of course, it was expected.'

'So I've been told.'

'Mr David had given up all his life to him, and I really believed he might have gone under when at last it happened. But no, he did the right thing, he filled the house with young men, the young men that poor Jeremy was never to join.' Mrs Dermott wiped away a tear.

Very sad, agreed Paddy to herself, only it was not the entire reason. I was.

'Mr David,' she observed aloud, 'was very fortunate to get four boys who shared his interests.'

'But my dear, once you see the stud you'll know it would be impossible not to be interested. I even think Mr David was hoping for a banana grower among them instead, he has a plantation down the mountains, but so far it's all horses.'

'Yes, adolescent boys ... also girls ... are like that,' Paddy agreed.

'But no girls here. A strictly male staff.'

'Yes, I would imagine Mr David would insist on that.'

'Likely he would, but it was the same with Kip Norris. Kip was Mr David's trainer—very skilled, got wonderful results.'

'He left?' inquired Paddy.

'Yes.'

'And he, too, was a woman-hater?'

'Oh, heavens, no!' Mrs Dermott laughed. 'You ask the valley girls. No, I think it was that Kip had to do everything himself, he would never—what's the word?'

'Delegate?'

'Yes. He refused to put anyone on, but as soon as he got out Mr David rectified that.'

'With four wards.' Paddy's voice was cold.

'Oh, no, he put others on as well.'

'With as much success as this Kip Norris?'

'It remains to be seen. Kip Norris was a wizard with horses, no doubt about that. It will be interesting to see how things go now.'

'At Yoothamurra?'

'Well, actually I was thinking of Standen Stud, the only comparable plateau property. That's where Kip went.'

'More wages, I expect,' Paddy commented.

'I admit I wondered about that, too. But I can't imagine Mr David letting someone go just for the sake of more money. However' ... a shrug ... 'Kip still went. Now if you don't mind, dear, I'll go, too. I only need to do the unit twice a week, Mr David has his own man who does his side, and I bring the boys' food in of a morning all ready to be heated up at night.'

'That's unnecessary now,' Paddy assured her. 'I can take over.'

'You'll be taking the boys over, something you know more about than I do, for we had no boys, only the one girl, and she's married and left now.'

'But what am I to do?' Paddy protested.

'I guess you'll fill in a week just looking around. Then after that there's the plantation, though you'll have to be taken there.'

'But do?' persisted Paddy. 'Do, not see?'

Mrs Dermott smiled.

'You ask the boys,' she shrugged. 'Also——'

'Yes?'

'You visit the stud.' Now her smile stretched all the way. She picked up her things, looked around to see if anything was left undone, then went out.

She might, thought Paddy, have left the washing up at least, but that was now sitting in a throbbing dishwasher. The house had every convenience. Paddy went to the big fridge and saw that it was stacked with pre-cooked dishes ready to be heated and served. Leaving, she shrugged, only her own bed to be closed up, for she was that kind of sleeper once she got off, and she had got off very quickly last night.

Well, seeing there was nothing else, she would do the closing up, then take a walk.

She strolled out of the back door a few minutes later to a large, immaculate lawn filled with tended plots of flowers and shrubs. She had not expected this, she had sensed a formal garden when they had pulled up last night at the front of the house, but she had thought that the rear would have been bare, probably cemented, strictly utilitarian as suited a stud. But there was no sign of any of the things that must go with a stud ... unless it was that string of outbuildings set well past a thick stand of native trees further to the rear.

She decided not to discover that yet, but to look around generally, and her first scrutiny was of the house itself. She walked along a stone path to the front.

It was indeed the castle she had said, and she could see her 'wing' dovetailed between Magnus David's side and the wards'. It was not a two-storeyed edifice, but it appeared so because of the basement that was taken over by garages. Paddy supposed that in the old days the carriages and sulkies had been deposited there.

She had reached the drive where he had halted last night, then announced: 'Madam, we've arrived.' It had been after he had answered her query as to why he obviously despised her so much with a tight:

'Because I loved him.'

Well, she understood all that now, but it did not make her feel any more warm towards him because of her understanding. She turned quickly, hoping he did not suddenly open the front door and descend the steps. Almost running in her agitation, she left the drive and chose a track to the right.

It proved heart-warmingly beautiful. There were no mountains to look at, for here was *on* the mountains, but there were rolling pastures as far as Paddy could see, and the grass, according to its age, ran a dazzling gamut of colour from emerald green to cigar and gold. The trees were in controlled thickets, mainly eucalypt, with the eucalypts' inimitable art of throwing lace patterns on the ground beneath.

A lot of the loveliness was in the air, apple-crisp, but with a hint of banana sweetness, for once over the plateau, Paddy knew now, the plantations opened up.

She crossed to a fence and climbed up to sit on it. As far as she could tell there was no one in whatever the fence was supposed to enclose, neither horse, nor livestock of any sort, nor gardener, stablehand, strapper. Then:

'Hi!' said a voice.

Paddy nearly fell off the fence in her surprise. She had looked around only a moment ago and seen nothing. Now there was a man, tall, blue-eyed, and somehow shining like the day was shining. He smiled at Paddy and said 'Hi' again.

'American?' Paddy smiled back of the 'Hi', for he was one of those people you had to smile at. 'Canadian?'

'Australian, but I've just returned from the States after selling one of our boys.'

'Boys?' she queried.

'Horses. Everything is horses here. I'm Kip Norris.' He extended a hand.

'Padua Travis, but don't let it frighten you, I'm usually called Paddy.'

'I like Padua. Welcome, Padua.'

'Thank you,' Paddy said. She said it warmly. It was the first glad-to-have-you gesture she had received. The boys, she had to admit, had not objected, but on the other hand they had not enthused, and as for Magnus David——

'But I'm puzzled,' Kip Norris was saying, 'as to where you sprang from.'

'Yoothamurra. I' ... a pause ... 'believe you know it.'

'Oh, yes, I know it,' he smiled. He had climbed to the top rail beside her. 'Don't tell me the great Magnus has taken on a girl strapper.'

'I was told by Mrs Dermott this morning that it could have been you who would never accept a female.' She had not been told quite that, Paddy knew, but just for fun she said it.

'Not under authority,' Kip Norris agreed, 'as I was under authority.'

'Under Mr David's authority?'

'Yes.' Kip Norris shrugged. However, his voice did not sound as resentful as it might have, Paddy thought, and she liked him for it.

'So you left Yoothamurra?' she asked.

'For the usual reason,' he nodded, 'that of bettering myself.'

'And have you?'

'I thought I had, but now, looking at you, realising what I've missed, I don't know.'

It was a charming compliment charmingly given by a charming man, and Paddy could not help feeling pleased.

The nice part was he didn't spoil it by following it up. He jumped down from the fence, raised his brows to her, and, when she nodded, put up his arms and lifted her down. He held her a moment longer than was necessary when she reached ground, but it was only a moment, an admiring moment, and she quite enjoyed it. He was *very* nice, she thought.

She would have liked to have found out his real reason for leaving Yoothamurra for an equal stud, for there must be a reason, but she still admired him for not speaking about it.

'Well, I'd better get back, see if there's work to do,' she said.

'Work ... then you're not a guest?'

'I'm an employee.'

'Then he did take on a girl strapper?'

'No,' she explained. 'I've come under a different category. I'm a house-mother. There are now four wards.'

'Yes, I heard about that.' He was looking at her with his smiling blue eyes, and once more Paddy smiled back.

'Lucky wards,' he envied.

'You don't know, I may be a gorgon.'

'Not with a face like yours, all the flowers of spring.'

'You do say nice things,' she protested.

'And you don't like them?' he asked of the protest.

'I ... well, I don't know whether I should accept them. I don't know you yet, do I?'

'I know you.'

She felt she knew him, too, but caution made her bring Magnus David into it.

'The big boss mightn't like it,' she said. She added: 'I almost called him Big Brother.'

'He was both once. A pity about Jeremy.'

'Yes.'

'You knew him?'

'Just knew him,' Paddy answered. Well, that was true.

'That's the way life goes,' Kip Norris shrugged. 'I only hope the kid fitted in all he could while he could. That's what I intend doing. No, Miss All the Flowers of Spring, I agree with you, Big Brother mightn't like it, so I wouldn't tell him if I were you.'

'The name is Padua, and I won't.'

'Goodbye, Padua.'

'Goodbye, Kip.' A few steps, then Paddy turned impulsively. 'Will I see you here again?'

'This is still Yoothamurra, make it further along the track to Standen.' He pointed to a cluster of buildings beyond some more thickets of eucalypts.

Paddy considered that, thought 'Why not?' and agreed.

This time she did go, and as she sauntered back towards the 'castle', she was pleasantly aware of his eyes on her, and, because she was a woman, she knew they were admiring eyes, admiring her ... and she liked that, too.

It was only when she came to a bend in the lane that she turned to see if he was still there, but he was gone.

When she turned back again there *was* someone ... Magnus David. He stood quite suddenly in front of her, evidently waiting for her recognition of him, then her attention.

He looked ... characteristically, Paddy thought, feeling she was now knowledgeable about the man ... annoyed.

CHAPTER FIVE

'WHAT in tarnation was attracting you back there?' Magnus David demanded suspiciously.

'I thought you were out on exercise—the boys said you were taking them, and Mrs Dermott even packed cut lunches.' Paddy spoke as shortly as he had, ignoring his question.

'Were you talking to someone? Did you see someone?'

'Where are the boys now?'

'Miss Travis, *I am speaking to you.*'

'And I'm speaking to you. I'm asking about the boys. They are in my care, remember, I'm their house-mother.'

'And I'm your boss. Answer me at once. With whom were you staging a rendezvous just now?'

Paddy said coldly, 'A rendezvous is an arranged meeting. Seeing I've barely arrived here wouldn't that be rather hard to achieve so soon?'

'You are taking obvious pains to evade me, meaning you did meet someone.'

'No, I did not!' In her indignation against this impossible man Paddy found the lie quite easy. She added: 'Satisfied now?'

'No. That was a very long backward glance.'

Paddy did not know what inspired her to offer: 'It's country worthy of a very long backward glance,' but she succeeded in instantly diverting him. At once his mood changed. He looked where she had been looking ... no sign of Kip Norris ... and his eyes flicked. He loves it, Paddy thought, and no wonder; it's a very beautiful corner.

'I did not go out with the boys,' he offered quite amiably, no doubt mollified by her praise, 'because I had a last-minute job to attend to. But I sent them along.'

'Are they capable?' she asked.

'Of course, otherwise they wouldn't have been allowed to go.'

'Then they could ride before they came here? You chose them because of that?'

'They could ride a merry-go-round steed, I'd say, but that would be all. No, I taught them.'

'But surely riding, responsible riding, which I imagine would be all you would go in for——'

'I certainly would!'

'Couldn't be taught in this short a time.'

'It can, and it has been, with' ... a reminiscent grin ... 'a lot of application.'

'On both sides?'

'Of course.'

Paddy asked, 'What if you'd got a non-rider among them?'

'It didn't happen.'

'But what if it had?'

'It didn't happen,' he continued, 'not after I took them to the stud.'

'Oh, that stud!' Paddy spoke impatiently. Mrs Dermott had said practically the same, she thought, anyone would think it contained some magic.

'After that, they couldn't wait to be shown,' went on

Magnus David. A pause. 'You ride, of course?'

'No "of course".'

'Then we must see to it, mustn't we?'

'No, we must not ... I mean, we need not. After all, I'm here in the role of house-mother, not rider.'

'However,' he insisted, 'I wish you to ride since the boys ride.'

For all the angry answers she had for him, Paddy found she could only murmur a plaintive: 'I'd never learn.'

'You'd learn as they did, with application on both sides.' He waited meaningfully. 'Day after day.'

'Day after day?'

'You don't catch on at one short lesson,' he told her.

'Mr David, there is no need for me to ride.'

'I think there is. You're here to watch over the wards, and the wards are more in the saddle than not.'

'Only because you've arranged it that way.'

'What if I have? It's a good healthy way.'

'And a good financial way too?'

'Meaning I'm enjoying cheap labour,' he nodded calmly. 'I've been waiting for that.'

'Well, aren't you?'

'Perhaps, and I'm not averse to it, but I didn't plan it.'

'Only connived at it?' she said sharply.

'Look, I simply took the youngsters over Yoothamurra and they were lost from then on.'

'Even to the extent of a saddle in the recreation room.'

He laughed at that ... and somewhere in the laughter Paddy found she had to join him. It *had* been funny, she recalled.

'All the same——' she tried to insert sternly.

'All the same, you'll be the same yourself after the

tour of inspection I now propose to give you.'

'Oh, no, I won't.'

'Won't be the same?'

'No, Mr David, I won't go on any tour of inspection with you. I'm here to house-mother, not to——'

The last words were broken off in incredulous indignation. The wretched man must have had his horse cropping in the thicket beside the track, for he had pulled on a rein she had not noticed before, mounted, then, before she could realise what was happening had lifted her up after him and propped her in front of him on the tall bay.

'Giddup, Sunset!' he urged.

'You——'

'Hold tight, I never believe in going round when I can go over.' Over a fence they went.

It wasn't far, for which Paddy was extremely grateful, but the short distance also gave her no time to regain her temper.

'You're quite impossible!' She was on her feet again now and trying vainly to straighten her crumpled dress. 'That jump——'

'We would have taken half an hour doing it the formal way,' he pointed out, 'because I would have had to let you down each time to open and shut a gate.'

'That's for when you're in cars.'

'It's also adopted for horseback if the rider behind the passenger decrees it.'

Decrees! Paddy fumed.

'Did the tour have to be now?' she asked tartly. 'And why couldn't we have walked?'

'It had to be now because I'm a busy man, also walking cuts into time.' He was tethering Sunset. 'Follow me, please.' He cut short the fresh argument he must have seen blazing in Paddy's face.

After a vexed hesitation, Paddy followed.

It was a perfectly maintained stud; Paddy, for all her bias, could see that at once. It comprised several neat rows of buildings, all serving a designed purpose.

'Farrier's shop,' indicated Magnus David, 'there's one for each building. Sand rolls.' He was walking crisply, and Paddy had to hurry to keep up with him, 'for after their dip in the pool. Pool's over there.' He pointed to a shining rectangle of water, as good as any human pool but different in its construction, for it was much deeper and its sides steeper, and instead of steps there was a ramp. 'Occasionally we take the fellers to the coast,' Magnus told her. 'It's not too far and there's nothing a horse likes better than catching a wave.

'Kitchen.' They were passing another building now. 'No, not for the hands but for the horses. Magic formulas are concocted in there—glucose, iron, calcium, secret ingredients to achieve astonishing results.'

He walked on. 'Fodder,' he said next. 'Dispensary. Surgery.'

'Delivery room?' Paddy came in pertly, hoping to catch him out.

'Yes, we have one, of course, though Yoothamurra soon found, like other studs, that the most successful labours turn out to be the natural ones in the field. Indeed, most mares refuse to foal elsewhere.

'This is how I instruct the boys to maintain a stable.' He had turned her into a large box, then followed.

Sweet and clean. They were the first words that came to Paddy. She drew a deep breath in pleasure, and hoped he did not notice it. It was all perfectly arranged and perfectly kept. In the storage corner, safely out of the reach of a curious horse who might harm itself, was a barrow, shovel, broom and fork, neatly stacked. Straw was distributed evenly over the surface, but pushed higher round the four walls against injury. A window was set at a right height.

'Very comfortable.' Paddy's voice came stiffly; she was afraid that if she did not hold herself aloof she would enthuse, and she had no intention of enthusing to this man.

Magnus David raised his brows at her curt commendation, then took her out and led her to a small walking ring. She saw several hands leading horses but she did not see the boys, so asked about them.

'I told you they were on an exercise. They'll be away all the morning. This is not a track, of course, it's just a first limber-up. After they do a few rounds they'll go on to the smaller trial track.'

'Little by little,' she agreed, still in the tight voice.

He glanced obliquely at her, then said: 'Yes, little by little, I'm a believer in that. Well, I think that's all, except——'

'Except?'

For answer he nodded for Paddy to follow him.

She did not go entirely unwillingly, though she was still determined to conceal any interest. Already she could see why the boys had been won over ... why, if she did not hold back she could be won over herself. It was the sweetness and cleanness of everything, it was the magnificence of gentle, magnificent animals. But no, she was not going to be won, Mr David.

As he walked, Magnus David talked.

'Mark, our fifteen-year-old' ... *our?* ... 'has all the early signs of a good breaker.'

'Horse-breaker?'

61

'Yes. He has the hands.' He stopped abruptly, stopping Paddy with him. He took her hands and examined them.

Still holding them, consciously or unconsciously Paddy did not know, he went on.

'The fellers are wild and raw when they come here, and then it starts. The blindfold over the near side eye to teach a horse not to kick, the first feel of the bridle, the most important rule of all: "Teach, not force." '

'And Mark has this gift?' Paddy released herself from his grasp.

'Yes.' Magnus had started walking again, so Paddy walked, too. She walked beside him to a small fenced paddock, then looked where he was looking.

It was a nice enough mare that he indicated, and the foal beside her was nice enough, too, but surely nothing to bring her over especially to see.

'She's blind,' he said.

'Blind?'

'The mare Melisande can't see her foal. Look, I'll bring her up.' He climbed the fence and walked to the mare. Paddy, who had noted that the small field was empty except for the mother and child, understood why now.

Magnus David took hold of the mare and enticed Melisande across to the rail. The little foal came, too. When Melisande was close, Magnus indicated two blank, cream-coloured eyes without any flicker or ripple of movement.

'She was born blind. Useless horseflesh, one might have said, except that she's an excellent mother. Instead of impairing her ability to produce good foals, it seems to have enhanced it. We first knew by accident ... oh, yes, these illegitimate births do occur at times even in the best regulated studs. To our embarrassment Melisande

62

dropped a foal by Big Harry, one-time Melbourne Cup winner, and a paying guest here for a resting season. About to remove the atom for its own safety, we saw that Melisande could manage very well, thank you.'

'But how? *How?*' asked Paddy.

'I'll never know. I think she has some sort of built-in antenna. Also, apart from never hurting a small one, she never hurts herself. She always pulls up within a few feet of danger.'

'And her foal——'

'Over-mothered,' grinned Magnus David. 'The young 'uns are pretty fleet-footed at that age, but Mum keeps up with them, makes them mind their manners. I always keep Melisande in the same field, it's the least I can do, and I vow she knows every tuft of grass. Indeed, nothing worries her so long as she can hear her child. Silence from baby is the only time she'll panic. If she can't hear anything she'll run in circles to disturb the little one in whatever it's doing to make it look up and catch up.'

'It's wonderful.' Paddy had to say it. She felt his eyes on her now, not on the blind mare, and she turned away, trying to conceal her emotion at the sightless mother.

He was looking quizzically at her. 'Well, that at least took some of the starch out of you,' he said.

'It's very kind of you to show me.' His words had stiffened her again, and taking her withdrawal as a cue for himself, he shrugged.

'Not so kind, I do quite well out of her. She's an excellent parent.'

That was more in keeping with the man she believed she knew. Paddy asked coolly: 'From what you've said I gather this foal is not Melisande's first?'

'No, that was Big Harry's boy—I told you. Also the

shining hope of Yoothamurra, our candidate for the Golden Downs Cup and the Plantation Plate. I'll give you one look only, he's precious stuff.' He was fairly running back to the stables, and if Paddy had had to hurry before, now she fairly raced.

He opened up a door of a stable and stood back as Paddy looked in.

The horse was barely brown, more the polished colour of young acorns. It had incredibly soft, dark-gold eyes. It was beautiful. It was heartwarmingly beautiful from its soft ears to its agile, flicking feet. It came straight to Paddy and nuzzled her, and she was aware and un-ashamed of tears pricking her eyes, stealing down her cheeks.

'He's lovely.'

'And an error. Not so the foal, she came from Quick as Lightning, another Cup winner, but she was planned. She has no name yet, but this boy is Into the Light. He was to have been called Son of Darkness, or something of the sort, but I stood out for the other.'

Into the Light. The sun came muted into the brown box, because of the higher-set window it sent amber shadows around the walls, a kind of amber nimbus. All at once Paddy was closing her eyes, feeling a strange rush of something she had never known before, and could not have explained now ... a kind of inexplicable sweetness.

Into the Light. She was opening her eyes again and meeting Magnus David's eyes, meeting them with a half-question ... turning her own glance away before he could answer that question, turning into the light again of the world outside.

'Inspection concluded,' she heard him say as though

a long way off. 'Do you want me to return you to the house?'

'Not if it's the same way as I came.'

'It would have to be if you can't ride. Now by this time next week . . .'

'I'll walk, thank you.' Without another word, Paddy started off.

As she passed the small paddock she saw the blind Melisande and the little foal cantering together. She walked to the railing and called to the mare, and it came over. She fondled its nose, told her she had just seen its firstborn and he was a fine fellow. Then, conscious that someone was watching her, she set quickly off again, not turning round for a full minute to check.

When she did turn round she could have cried with annoyance that she had done so. For Magnus David was still standing by the fodder room watching her. Watching her turn round to see him, no doubt.

This time Paddy did not turn until she reached the house.

It was a very quiet house without the wards. Without the boss, too, she supposed, for the little she had to do with him so far had given no indication of his being a silent man. Far from it, she thought ruefully. She listened for sounds of the man who did for him now doing for him, but could hear nothing. She turned her attention to her own régime.

She would have liked to have known more about the boys. According to her Closer Families training it was the only way a house-mother could become closer. She decided to study their room with the idea of learning something of their personalities, not a very bright idea, she knew, when she did not know which bed served which, but ... and a smile ... at least she would be aware of Jockey Paul's corner, because his pyjamas would be smaller. About to try this, Paddy saw an envelope on the floor at the door that led into Magnus David's side, and crossed and took it up. There was no note, but the contents contained potted histories of each of the four, so good marks at least, Mr David, Paddy awarded, for that.

She made a jug of coffee and sat at the table and studied the notes. All four, she ascertained, were orphans. Deliberate on David's part, or had it simply happened like that? If the wards' parents were still alive, then that ruled out any likelihood of uninterrupted guardianship, but if they were parentless, then the guardian stood a good chance of retaining them for a long period. Very handy for Mr David, Paddy thought, putting aside a possibility that the boys might have turned out a liability and not an asset to him.

All four had gone through the accepted lower school grades quite satisfactorily, though none had shown any inclination to continue their studies to tertiary level. Of course not, snorted Paddy, Magnus David would not need a scientist or professor around the place.

You're being unfair, a little deep down voice accused Paddy, but she refused to listen.

She saw that there were none of the obvious medical things to watch for, like spring colds, rashes from wool near the skin, red spots after strawberries or tendencies to bronchitis, and put the data down. How little *really* it all revealed. How much different it was with actual children than children written up in a book. *He* had said that, he had told her you could teach a man to fly on paper but he wouldn't like to be a passenger on the first take-off. Very wise, Mr David, she shrugged, only this take-off is going to be different, I'm going to make it succeed. It's going to be hard with a quartet of horse-obsessed juniors, but I'll still show you.

Though how, *how*? she wondered. She looked up at the pictures of the finishes of races, of framed winners decked in their colours, and, about to sigh, grinned instead. If you can't lick 'em, join 'em, she thought.

When the two youngest arrived back some hours later, followed soon after by the other pair, Paddy did just that.

They had dinner ... Paddy had only to heat it ... to the tune of the racing ability of Winged Beauty, half-sister to Roman Prince, compared to Billy Boy, brother of In Pursuit, and somewhere in the chatter Paddy found she was joining in, too. It made it easier for her to insert a few questions of her own as to where the seniors had ridden today, what they would study tonight ... oh, yes, they must study, who ever heard of a trainer who could not account for himself on paper. She asked the schoolboys their grades and their subjects.

It all went well.

After the meal she superintended homework and study until it was time for bed. To her surprise, for this was one thing psychology had not yet licked, they all went off cheerfully at her bidding. She soon learned why. Richard said:

'You have to have lashings of sleep when you're in this kind of job.'

She put their bathroom light out, put their dormitory light out, gave the unit a final check, then retired to her own suite. It was too early for bed for her, she thought; after all, she was no adolescent intending to train or ride or exercise a horse tomorrow.

'Psst!'

The sound came from the window, the window through which early this morning she had looked back at an eye. A boy again?

No, it was not a boy, it was Magnus David. He was hissing to her from his own window. Annoyed, for she hated being alerted like that, Paddy unwillingly went across.

'In bed?' he asked.

'The boys?'

'Well, not you,' he jeered.

'Then yes.'

'All well?'

'Naturally.'

'Very smug about it, aren't you?' he commented.

'No, just assured of my ability.'

'How nice.'

Paddy sighed. 'Did you hiss me over to say that?'

'No, to tell you that tomorrow we'll do the plantation.'

'Oh, yes, I'd like that.'

'I hadn't finished,' he went on. 'On horseback.'

'What?' she gasped.

'I think you heard me.'

'Yes, I heard you, but you can't be serious. I told you I'd never ridden, and it must be miles away.'

'Thirty kilometres by twisting road, five by eagle, eight along our track.'

'I couldn't do it,' Paddy protested.

'It's an excellent way to learn, it's a reasonable grade down.'

'But if we go down, we must come up,' she said dryly.

'Yes, but by then you'll be an experienced rider, Miss Travis, and take the stumps and fallen logs and roots and squelchy bits and outcrops like a veteran.'

'You can't be serious.'

'I'm very serious. I'm all for crash courses.'

'I *will* crash. I'm grown, I'm adult, not a child.'

'Only the companion of children,' he reminded her thinly, and by the thinness Paddy knew he was not referring to their wards but to Jerry, aged seventeen, yet she had thought ...

'You said little by little before.' She made a final bid for his mercy. 'You can't change it to a crash course.'

'As soon as the kids go off to school and off to work,' he said relentlessly. His voice was not so clear now, and she saw that he was withdrawing from the window. 'If you haven't any slacks, borrow a pair of Paul's pants.'

'I have slacks.'

'I'll be waiting round the back. Best to give you your first leg-up in private. If nothing else you must admit I'm considerate in that.'

Paddy was not sure about those last words; she had withdrawn herself, withdrawn in as massive a temper as she had ever known.

'I hate him! I won't go!' She said it to her four walls, thankful now for a separate unit so that she could say things aloud.

'I hate him. I won't go.'

The next morning Paddy still hated him ... but she went.

CHAPTER SIX

PADDY felt as much like a ride down a mountain as she felt like a sleep on a bed of nails. As a matter of fact the sleep, even on nails, sounded attractive, for she had not put the light out until the small hours, and she was tired.

Somewhere in the boys' unit, she had reasoned last night, there must be a riding manual, for these wards had known as much about horses when they had arrived here as she knew now. Perhaps their lessons had been entirely practical, but it had seemed likely, with two of the boys already making horses their career, that some data might be around. She had felt sure there would be notes, or hints, or guides, and after giving the wards an hour to reach the second deeper phase of sleep, Paddy had tiptoed into the dorm. She had found nothing lying around, but she did ... later ... in the adjoining recreation or hobby room. She had had a moment of panic when the books were under the saddle, and the saddle, upon the books' removal, fell noisily to the floor, but she need not have worried, the boys slept like logs.

At once she had taken the books to her room.

How To Approach Mount. She had read the chapter anxiously. She had skipped Care of, Grooming of, Health of—one of the hands would have attended to those items, but she did memorise the correct seat, the rein movements, the bodily response to the movement of the horse.

She read with interest that the cavalryman bent the leg to some extent, the Red Indian to a greater extent but that cowboys rode with a straight leg. She wondered which method was being adopted by the boys ... no, cancel that, any method of theirs would be the Magnus David speciality, *of course*. And how had he ridden? She really could not recollect, the only time she had seen him on horseback she had not seen him much, not crowded in front of him as she had been. Paddy had stiffened in humiliated memory.

She learned a jingle she considered helpful.

'Your head and your heart keep up.
 Your hands and your heels keep down.
 Your knees keep close to your horse's side,
 And your elbows close to your own.'

Passing over show jumping, which included frightening things like fences, double fences, walls and water, she came back to mounting, rapport with your mount and the rhyme. Most of all the rhyme.

'Your head and your heart keep up.' Paddy sat straight and proud.

'Your hands and your heels keep down.' She did this assiduously.

'Your knees keep close to your horse's side.' She made the sofa the horse.

'And your elbows close to your own.'

She read encouragingly that if this jingle was put into practice that an earnest applicant should be well on the way to becoming a rider.

On that assurance, she had at last gone to bed.

It was a bad beginning having so little sleep, but it was worse still when Magnus David met her as arranged the next morning then promptly sent her back to change.

'Change?' she echoed.

'That's what I said.'

'Change what? Shirt, slacks?' With impudence: 'Make-up?'

'Change your pants,' he ordered.

'To what?'

'To Paul's. Paul would be your size.'

'My size, but not my shape.'

'I'm aware of that, Miss Travis, but the boys have been provided with riding pants, and these pants differ vastly from ordinary slacks. More seat, a very necessary thing. In which case' ... with maddening estimation of Paddy ... 'you need not be concerned about any difference in shape, I think.'

Angrily Paddy said: 'What's wrong with these slacks?'

'Too tight in one place, too wide in another. The wide part is the legs. You're going riding, not sallying forth in bellbottoms to brave the waves.'

'I wish I was braving waves,' said Paddy bitterly. 'I wish I was anywhere but here.'

'You should have thought of that before, shouldn't you?'

'*I* think of it?'

'Remember September,' he said hatefully. 'Now get changed. Pronto!'

She had gone up and found a khaki pair of Paul's trews that went on but made her look like a walking balloon. She came down again.

'Satisfied?' she demanded.

'Yes.'

'Well, *I* think I look awful.'

He did not argue about that, which made her feel even more awful.

'This is Donna,' he introduced, and Paddy looked at the filly he had brought and at once felt a little better. She had not put it past this man to present a large edition like his mount was, or failing that a spirited, frisky one, but Donna seemed just right.

'Yes, she's reasonable,' he agreed, reading Paddy's thoughts. 'How much do you know?'

'Your head and your heart keep up——' she began, but he nodded before she could go on.

'I was started myself on that.'

'Many years ago,' she slipped in.

He looked at her sidewise. 'How many?'

'I already know. You told me. You were sixteen years older than Jerry.'

'Too old?' he asked.

'Too old for what?'

'That answers me,' he said enigmatically. 'Yes, it's a sound jingle, especially the head and the heart being up. Is yours up? No, never mind, get up. I presume you can mount.'

If crossed fingers could help her, Paddy knew she would mount. She approached Donna correctly, bit determinedly down on her lip, breathed hard ... and managed it.

'Excellent,' he praised. 'I rather expected you to bring out a chair.'

'As though I would!'

'Well, I knew you'd sooner do that than accept a hitch from me.'

'Shall we start?' she asked haughtily.

'Can you?'

Paddy gave Donna a reminding slap, a slap a little sharper in her indignation than she had intended, and Donna cantered off far too smartly for Paddy's liking.

'Serves you right.' Magnus David had caught up with

Paddy. 'Never, *never*, mind you, vent your bad temper on your friend.'

'Donna mightn't be my friend,' Paddy pointed out.

'I think she is, though. I instinctively think you like horseflesh. I saw your face yesterday when I showed you Into the Light.'

'Well, I was sorry as soon as I smacked her,' Paddy admitted.

'I could see that,' he said. 'You were scared.'

'But still sorry for Donna. It was your fault, picking on me.'

'If you're to learn you'll have to take criticism.'

'But not downright discouragement, surely.'

'Stop arguing and attend to what you're doing,' he snapped. 'You can't put all the onus of this ride on Donna, after all she's already got the burden of you.'

Paddy bit down on her lip again and attended.

It wasn't at all bad now she had begun, in fact it was quite pleasant. After the initial shock of being up from the ground and moving forward still up from the ground, Paddy began to enjoy it.

They went down the track she had walked yesterday, and seen from aloft it was even more superb.

She wondered if Kip Norris would be out, and if he was whether she should recognise him. It would make it awkward after yesterday's lie to Magnus. But there was no sign of Kip, no sign of anybody. There was the distinct presence of the neighbouring stud, though, and, remembering she was not supposed to know, Paddy asked Magnus about it.

'What are those buildings?' She pointed.

'They belong to our opposition.'

'Are there other studs up on the plateau?'

'A few, but Standen comprises our opposition.'

'And that's Standen?'

'It's Standen.' His lips were thinned, and he did not encourage any more of that.

'It's big,' Paddy persisted.

'Yoothamurra and Standen represent the big business, the smaller owners mostly have bloodstock only for a sideline,' he told her.

'You could say sideline about yourself,' Paddy pointed out, 'you also raise bananas.'

'For the horses.'

'I don't believe you.'

'Then begin believing. Just because an apple is the time-honoured fruit to give to a horse there's no reason to think that a banana would be unwelcome.'

'I've never seen a horse eating a banana.'

'Then you'll see. Know anything about this oldest fruit of all?'

'Only that it's not the oldest.'

'You're thinking of Eve.'

'Yes, I am.'

'Then Eve tempted Adam with a banana, or so they declare up here. Keep that in mind, Miss Travis, when you're in a tempting mood.'

She let that pass, but picked him up on his statement that he only grew bananas for fodder.

'No, you're right,' he agreed, 'I make a tidy profit out of it, but of course, I grow very good bananas. It was my parents' plantation, and after they passed on Uncle maintained it for when we ... I ... could take it over.'

'Handy that the stud and plantation were close,' said Paddy stiffly, deeply resenting that correction from 'we' to 'I'.

'But there was never any likelihood of them not being close. The parents of both my parents and my aunt's and uncle's parents came here in the year dot, and once you come, you never go.' He gave her a long oblique look.

They had left Standen behind them now and were cutting across an open field to a distinct break in the surrounding cliff edges. It looked as though it would be the beginning of a descent, and Paddy, who was doing very well now, shut her eyes a moment.

'All right?' he asked.

'Yes, but——' She nodded to where they were headed.

'You'll be all right, and once you get this over you'll be an accomplished rider.'

'I could have done without the accomplished part, just a rider would have done.' They were very near the edge now.

'It's worse coming up,' he assured her cheerfully. 'Don't be worried, Donna knows what it's all about.'

Donna did, and without Donna's knowledge Paddy knew she could never have made that giddy descent.

It came upon her suddenly. From clear level pasture they dropped into a snaky track descending between impeding trees, fallen logs and slippery rock outcrops. But it was the steepness that appalled Paddy; at times she felt she would have been better off dismissing Donna and coming down by a ladder. Yet he had described it as reasonable! How perverse, how deliberately hateful, could a man get?

'It levels out soon,' encouraged Magnus, who had gone ahead to catch her if she fell. Already he had told her: 'Coming back I'll stop behind to pick up the pieces.'

It was amazing how even before the levelling out Paddy got used to it. She actually found herself looking around. It was lovely, lush country, thick with trees hung with staghorns and wild orchid, full of sudden gorges and deep gulches, where waterfalls splayed out and smudgy shadows turned the air to a misty blue.

They were nearing the bottom now, and through the trees Paddy could see an old house.

'Empty,' Magnus told her. 'There's never been anyone living here since my parents had the plantation. The trees still thrive ... at least their children's children do, for that's how bananas function, the old palm has to make way for the new ... but the home is bereft. It's mostly that way out here now, plantationers live in the town and manage their plantations from there.'

'Yes,' said Paddy inattentively, for her eyes were on the battalions of bananas growing up the almost vertical cliffside, rows and rows of bananas, melting away the rugged edges and clothing them instead in sparkling green, green everywhere, except where the bright blue ripening bags blossomed out like giant cornflowers.

'Sodium, potassium, copper, all for the taking,' said Magnus of the heavy hanging hands, 'no wonder our horses thrive. You didn't believe me before, did you?' He reached out and picked a banana and presented it to Donna.

'Unpeeled?' asked Paddy.

'She's probably getting more iron like that. I don't know, I've never been into it, and certainly never tried it. While I cut a swag of them to take back, you look round the house.' He tossed her a key.

Paddy would have sooner stopped outside, the air was wonderful here, a combination of warm, enclosed valley and not-so-distant sea. But it seemed churlish to refuse. She climbed a few steps and let herself in.

77

The house might be empty, but it still lived. She felt that at once. The clock left on the old-fashioned mantelpiece ticked steadily, and it even muted Magnus's steps as he silently joined her where she stood.

'Yes,' he said, startling her, 'I keep it wound. Did I frighten you?'

'No. Yes.'

He smiled at that, but not a derisive smile this time. It must be the house, Paddy thought, it must do things like this to people like Magnus.

He became silent, too, now. There seemed only the pair of them, not just here in this empty house, but in the whole world. Paddy could not have explained how she felt, except that she was waiting somehow ... Waiting? Waiting for what?

Then she saw him take a step towards her, and she felt such a strange largeness in her heart that she knew she either had to step forward, too ... or step back.

She stepped back.

'I did frighten you.' His voice derided her now.

'No.'

'I think so. You're scared.'

'I'm not!' she denied.

'Then why are you withdrawing?'

'I'm not.'

'Then you're not advancing, are you? This is advancing.'

Before Paddy could realise what he was doing, he was pulling her to him and kissing her. Kissing her in a manner that left no indecision that she had been kissed. Yet there was no fulfilment to the kiss, and there was no emotion. He—he was giving her a lesson, that was how it felt. At last he let her go, and she went and stood by the table.

'What was that for?' she asked jerkily.

'Do you have to have a reason? Did you ... at Pelican Beach?'

'I didn't ... we didn't ...' But she did not go on. What was the use ... ever ... with a man like this?

'Aren't you finished yet?' she asked.

'I've checked what has to be checked and picked us some fruit.'

'Then you have finished.'

'It all depends,' he drawled, 'on what you expected me to do.'

Paddy felt like retorting:

'I expected at least for you not to lose our first footing of friendship. We had it for a moment when you entered the house. Why did you do what you just did?'

Instead she said:

'When you're ready, I am.'

Magnus hesitated, hesitated for such a brief second it might not have been hesitation at all, then he led the way to the door. It was only as she was descending the steps that Paddy noticed the hamper—a well-packed picnic hamper. She even could see a bottle of wine. Well, if he had wanted to eat down here, why hadn't he said?

She crossed again to Donna.

The climb up again was hazardous, but Paddy took it well. She had other things on her mind, and that helped. They reached the top and began the canter over the plateau. As they passed Standen, a figure emerged from one of the outbuildings, and even across the paddock Paddy saw that it was Kip.

Kip did not recognise her in any way, and Paddy did the same with him. She found herself quite enjoying the conspiracy, even though it was foreign to her nature. Anything, *anything*, she was smouldering, to confound or annoy or—or hurt this hurting man.

'You know, Travis, for all that I passed it over yesterday I still rather suspected that you'd met Norris.' Magnus was a little ahead of her and he tossed it back at Paddy.

'Then you suspected wrongly,' she lied.

'Yes, and that suits me. Standen and Yoothamurra have no time for each other. When Norris left us for them he knew that.'

'Interesting,' said Paddy.

He firmed his lips at her polite impoliteness, but when they reached the house, he spoke again.

'Something else interesting. I brought it from the plantation house. My mother's old banana cookbook. As you're a woman I thought you might like to take a look.'

As you're a woman. Paddy stiffened. What else 'as a woman' was she expected to accept? A man taking a step towards you and kissing you, then laughing ... not literally but still laughing ... in your face?

Had that been simply because she was a woman? To his warped way of thinking a woman to be taught a lesson? Was it because of Jerry?

Oh, Jerry, she thought wistfully, remember September, remember spring, everything young and untried and uninvolved? Not like this. But that was you, Jerry, not your brother.

She dismounted and left Donna in Magnus's care and went into the house.

CHAPTER SEVEN

THE cookbook could have been a portent of what was to come, but Paddy was not to meet that situation until a week later.

During that week she got to know her family, from the usual wards' distrust of anyone outside their tight circle to their inherent thrift. Yes, thrift. Thrift was something they all eventually achieved. House-mothers and house-fathers perforce preached it—they had to. Every cent saved meant more wards, or more care for the existing ones, it was pumped into the children as soon as they arrived and every day after. Paddy smiled fondly and knowledgeably when she saw the pickaback soap. No wastage when a cake of soap grew thin, the thin wedge was pressed on to a new cake. It was always thus. She was looking at the three colours of the present soap when Magnus David strolled in one morning. Whatever else he had come to say was brushed aside.

'What in Betsy is that?' he demanded.

'Pickaback soap.'

'Pickaback soap! A new product?'

'As old as the hills,' Paddy assured him.

'The hills here are very old, the terrain has been established as the oldest in the world.'

'Then still as old, for I guess there were orphans at the time of the first Java men.'

'And they economized with pickaback soap?'

'Yes. It's one of the many things that's instilled at an early age, as is turning off unnecessary lights, for instance, using half the amount of toothpaste.'

'It's a pity,' Magnus grunted, 'other economies were not introduced. Like fillet steak and scrag, for example.'

'I beg your pardon?'

'Richard was sent up from the cold storage with the household meat. It's also his duty to feed the various domestic animals.'—There were several dogs and cats.

'I think I can guess what's coming,' grinned Paddy. 'In his inattention or absorption with something else——'

'Inattention is my word.'

'He gave the cats and dogs the fillet and left you the scrag. Well, no worry to us, Mrs Dermott brings our meals ready to be heated.'

'But not mine.'

'No, your man does that.'—Come to think of it, Paddy had never seen any man.

'When I don't eat down at the stables, I fend for myself.'

'But Mrs Dermott said——'

'I know, but I didn't want a woman fussing around.'

'But you'll have to, won't you, when you marry.'

'At the present I'm not contemplating marriage,' he assured her.

'I see. Well, I'm sorry I can't help you with the scrag, but I'm sure slow cooking would do the trick. Perhaps your mother's book——'

'It deals with bananas. I thought you would have discovered that by now.'

'I've been very busy,' she said coldly. 'Would you like to take one of Mrs Dermott's ready-to-be-heateds from us?'

'No, I'll eat down at the stud again. I'll have to quite soon, anyway. We are expecting a blessed event. How do you feel about parent participation?'

Paddy thought she knew what he was about to say, but chose to feign dumbness.

'The stallion is going to be present, then?' she asked archly.

'I'm intending to have the boys there. Not parents, but so involved they could be considered close relatives at least.' He awaited her comment.

She nodded, deliberately not paying it much interest, but he repeated his question, evidently needing a definite answer.

'Participation?' he asked.

'If you say so.'

'I do say so. It's never too early to sort out the boys from the men.'

'It's usually the other way about, and I don't agree that any who fail your test are less male for that.'

'Spoken admirably, Miss Travis, but I didn't mean it quite so stringently. What I want them to realise is that it's not all roses.'

'Roses?' she queried.

'They're keen now, but eight nights in a cold paddock, and it can get cold up here, can sometimes break down enthusiasm.'

'Eight nights?' Paddy gasped.

'Little Lulu, our mother-to-be, took that long last time, took eight chilly, watching nights. I'm hoping for a quicker performance this go, but it still remains to be seen. I believe some of them could change their minds.'

'Embrace bananas instead, you mean? That would suit you, wouldn't it? You would have both projects safely staffed.'

Magnus was looking coldly across at her from the other side of the boys' bathroom where he had found her tidying up after the morning showers. Paddy still held the pickaback soap.

'Has anyone ever told you,' he asked, 'that you are an exceptionally objectionable female?'

'Yes—you. Just now.'

'No one else?'

'Give them time,' she said insolently, and went to flounce out, then stopped. He stood blocking the door and his feet were set very firm.

'Do you know what I'd like to do to you?' he said. 'I'd like to turn the shower on you good and hard.'

'Cold, of course.'

'Of course.'

'Then why not the horse pool?' she suggested. 'The water's there already, and I could finish with a sand roll.'

'That's only for the thoroughbreds, Miss Travis.' He had stepped forward as he spoke and it allowed a few inches for Paddy to escape. She did so, but just. She went into her own unit and turned the key. A hateful man! 'Only for the thoroughbreds.' Why didn't he reach his decision on her ... his *pre*-decision ... and get the agony over? Found wanting, she thought, and suddenly wanting herself, wanting companionship not criticism, she decided to try to see Kip Norris again. Kip had wanted them to meet up, he had told her so. He had not said when, but he would be looking out for her, she felt sure of that. She would wait until she heard Magnus David leave the house, until she made sure by peering out that he was making for the stud, then she would go down the track. Several minutes later it happened like that.

Paddy went straight up the track she had taken before, but she walked much further this time, past the fence that marked the boundary between the two studs ... the opposition, Magnus had called it ... then to a point where the Standen stables began. Scarcely had she reached the first one than Kip Norris emerged like a spontaneous Jack-in-the-box.

'Padua!' he greeted.

He looked very handsome with the sun shining on his thick fair hair but more than his outstanding good looks Paddy was warmed by his bright, welcoming smile. After Magnus David's dourness it came like sun after rain. With the smile came his extended hand and when Paddy put her own into the well-manicured one ... how nice to care about your appearance in an outdoor job like his! ... she did not mind that he kept it there.

Smiling back at him, she said: 'You appeared out of that barn as though you've been waiting all the week.'

'I have.'

'Oh, Kip!'

'Well, perhaps not, Padua, but I have looked out every day.'

'I did go past once,' she told him.

'With David. I was glad you made no sign of recognition. You were a smart girl.'

'I had to make no sign—he'd questioned me, and I had said I hadn't met you.'

'*Very* smart girl.' He still held her hand.

'It seemed awful, though,' she confessed, 'I mean, I don't tell lies.'

'You don't have to tell me that with a face like yours.'

'And what is that?'

'I told you last time—all the flowers of spring.'

'Oh, Kip!' she said again, but secretly she was flattered and pleased.

'Were you coming from the plantation?' Kip asked.

'Yes.'

'Lucky man, Magnus, not only a leading stud but a profitable banana farm. And all to himself, now.'

'Unhappily,' inserted Paddy.

'Yes, unhappily,' Kip was quick to agree. 'However,' he added, 'his brother's passing did fill Magnus's coffers to overflowing.'

'Well, perhaps it did, yet perhaps not.' Paddy did not know what prompted that remark, for the subject was certainly something she never thought about.

'What do you mean, Padua?' Kip asked.

She tumbled out her story. Well, why not? Kip was her friend, and she had no other friend here. Mrs Dermott was nice but busy with her own life, and the boys were just that, boys. In her excuses to herself for spilling something that probably would have been better not spilled, Paddy did not look up at Kip Norris. If she had she might have seen an estimating look in Norris's eyes.

'Left to you!' he marvelled.

'Yes. We ... Jerry and I ... met at Pelican. I never guessed, I never knew ...'

'No, of course not.' His reassurance came warm and comforting, so different from Magnus David's cold suspicious comments. 'How could you know? But what now?'

'Nothing now, of course. He ... Magnus David ... despises me. I just can't fathom why he bothers to pretend to look me over, unless it's curiosity. His decision was made before he even saw me.'

'You could object, you know, and I think you'd have a damn good case. After all, a man's last will and testament——'

'But Jerry was a child and I was little more than one.'

'But a clever legal man——'

'Kip, I don't want the wretched money,' she sighed.

'Not now, but you may one day. You may even marry someone to whom a helping hand in the way of a nice round sum could put him in business, begin the pair of you on the road to affluence, help all round.'

'I suppose you're right, but——'

'I am right.'

'But I still wouldn't consider it.'

'No, of course not, never you, All the Flowers of Spring,' Kip said quickly and smoothly. 'Let's leave that mundane subject and talk about something very near to my heart—no, not you.' He smiled charmingly. 'You are, you know, already you are, but I would never tell you so this soon.'

'Oh, Kip, you are a fool!' Paddy laughed.

'A nice fool, I hope?'

'Very nice. But what, apart from me' ... a quirk ... 'is near to your heart?'

'The boys and girls back there.' Kip nodded to Yoothamurra. 'Somehow I've never got to love this bunch as I loved that. No, Padua, not the hands, the boys and the girls with _four_ feet, not two. The stallions, geldings, mares, colts, fillies. How are they?'

'Fine,' Paddy assured him.

'And the blind mare, has she foaled yet?'

'Oh, yes, her daughter is quite leggy.'

'And ... the precious firstborn? The house speciality? Son of Darkness?'

'Oh, no, not that name!' Paddy was shocked.

'No, of course not.' Again Kip came in at once. 'I never

liked it, anyway. I wanted another name, but David said——'

'Did he?' Magnus had put it the other way round, Paddy thought, but then Magnus would. 'Well, he must have had second thoughts. He's now Into the Light.'

'Ah!' smiled Kip appreciatively. He pressed her hand.

They stood for quite a while with their hands locked.

'Why did you leave Yoothamurra, Kip?' Paddy asked presently.

'One of those things. He never dismissed me and I never walked out on him. It just dissolved, I guess you could say. I simply found myself preferring to work here.'

'More wages?'

'Let's say greater prospects. But let's not talk about me any more, Padua. Would you like to come into Standen and look around?'

'Not now,' she said. 'I only came out on impulse.'

'An appreciated impulse.'

'Appreciated, too, by me. Mr David and I had had a few words. I just felt I must get out.'

'Keep feeling like that, and every time I'll be waiting. By the way, Padua, after you put your kids to bed of a night is your day's work over?'

'Well, yes, I think it should be.'

'Then why not come across to the club with me some time? The Plateau Club, quite tasteful. It will be mostly horse talk you'll hear, but not, I promise, at our table.'

'And what talk there?' she smiled.

'Come and hear. It's quite nice—good décor, a small but excellent orchestra. In a minor way the city come to the bush.'

'I like the bush,' Paddy confided.

'And you'll like the club. Will you?'

'Does he go?' she asked.

'He does not. Not his cup of tea at all.'

'Is that why you're asking me? Because you know you won't see him?'

'I'm asking you because I want you,' Kip said firmly. 'But his absence, I must admit, makes it more attractive. And after all, why shouldn't you step out?'

'Why shouldn't I?' Paddy agreed. She said regretfully: 'I really must go now.'

'Then till next time. Say that for me.'

'Till next time,' smiled Paddy, and she turned and walked back to Yoothamurra.

The break had done her good, and she set to heating up the prepared meal that the boys would be looking forward to the moment they got in.

She emptied the jars into saucepans, then stacked the jars for Mrs Dermott to take back when she came tomorrow with fresh supplies. What a life, she smiled— she had not been called upon to cook once. Still ... picking up the banana book ... she wouldn't have minded trying her hand.

When the wards arrived, though the meal was as appetising as Mrs Dermott always made it, they did not do it justice. Paddy supposed that the two stableboys had over-eaten at lunch, and as for the schoolboys ... well, everyone knew schoolboys.

'Have you a tuckshop?' she asked them, suspecting a sweet feast during the day.

No, no tuck, nothing at all, it was just a one-room school in the valley, no shops, no stalls. Paddy, at a nod from the seniors, decided to believe that. She asked more questions but only got brief answers, not because of any secrecy, she thought, but because they were tired. The older ones looked tired, too. But teenage boys were never tired, she frowned.

There was no trouble in getting them to bed, indeed they were eager to go, and Paddy was putting out the unit lights and preparing to go to her own quarters when the telephone rang.

It was the first time it had pealed, and she crossed the room and took up the receiver suspiciously. She knew that the main connection was to the master flat, and that any calls had to be put through from there. Surely Kip had not rung up to fix up a definite date for the club? It would be embarrassing talking to him when one knew that two listened. Not necessarily perhaps, but Paddy still felt that Magnus David would do just that.

But it was not Kip asking David could he be put through, it was Magnus David himself.

'Miss Travis?'

'Yes.'—Who else could he think it was?

'I've had a message from Mrs Dermott.'

'Yes?'

'She's ill,' he told her. 'Can't attend in the morning.'

'Oh, that will be all right,' said Paddy.

'I haven't finished. It's likely she'll be unable to attend all the week. She's come down with that new virus that has reached the north coast, one that I hoped they'd keep down there, not send up to the plateau.'

'You mean there are more cases?'

'So I've been told, and still more expected. It's a really vicious strain. I only hope we can keep the wretched thing down.'

'Can it spread to the stables?'

'No, man can't transmit his diseases there, nor horses

to man, but if the hands go down it's going to be hard. Most of all I want the boys to miss it if at all possible. Any suggestions?'

'Well,' said Paddy, 'the two schoolboys could stay at home—germs spread through classes like wildfire. But I doubt if they'll want that, they quite seem to like their school, even though they weren't very communicative tonight.'

'What's that?' sharply.

'They went to bed early, the whole four of them,' she explained.

'Oh, lor'!'

'But don't worry yet, the young ... and after all, they still are very young ... recuperate quickly. Why, by tomorrow——'

But by the next day the four were laid low. Pains, cramps, aches, nausea, the whole bit.

When he came in at night to ask Paddy if she considered it absolutely necessary for the coast doctor to come up as he was already cruelly overworked, Magnus David looked so worn that Paddy caught her breath.

'You really should be in bed yourself,' she said.

'Can't. We're shockingly under-staffed.'

'Can't you get anyone in?'

'All the studs are suffering the same.'

'... Standen?'

'Probably.'

'They mightn't be.'

'No, but I'd never ask them.'

'That's foolish,' said Paddy. 'A Kip Norris worked here once, so I've been told, so surely he'd work again ... that is, unless he's gone down, too.'

'I will not have Norris,' snapped Magnus. 'Understood? I think you're right, I think I am going to be under the weather for a while, but that's still my last word, Miss Travis. No Norris. Understood?'

'It should be, you've said it twice.'

'No Norris—Three times. Now I'll leave you. Sorry to be no help to you, but it would be worse still if I stayed. Perhaps if I hit myself with lemon and rum——'

'No good at all,' said Paddy.

'Thank you for the advice, Doctor, but I will all the same.'

During the night Paddy heard him coughing, and because the boys were producing the same racking sounds she knew the worst.

When she got up, she checked, and yes, it was true. She had five patients on her hands.

CHAPTER EIGHT

REST and warmth—Paddy knew they were the two cardinal rules for 'flu, so she administered both relentlessly. She had no trouble with the boys. They were so sick not even a Melbourne Cup would have got them out of their beds, but she did, visiting Magnus later, have trouble there. Magnus, pale and drained, wobbly, hollow-eyed, still wanted to go across to the stud.

'You'll stay where you are,' Paddy ordered.

'You don't understand. The stables——'

'The stables are being well tended. No one has succumbed there yet.' It was a lie. Paddy had not been down to find out. 'The schoolboys must have brought the bugs from class,' she went on, 'and so far it's only confined here.' That was another lie, Paddy had heard that most of the plateau was infected.

'What about you?' Magnus mumbled weakly.

'I'm fine. I had preventive injections in Sydney.' Another lie, the 'flu was a new strain and no vaccine was available yet.

'I still think——'

'Drink this as you do so.' She put a hot toddy in his hand, laced with something else besides rum, a rather strong sedative. Well, rightly or wrongly she had to keep him in that bed.

He fell asleep almost at once, and when his breathing got quite profound, Paddy went back to her boys.

Sick as they were now, they were no trouble. They were a worry, though, and Paddy contacted the coast doctor, for there was no medico up here. A tired voice answered her. No, said Doctor Williams, he could not possibly get up, he had too much already on his plate here. Yes, hot lemon and aspirin, and if she was really alarmed then some antibiotic that Magnus David would no doubt have in his emergency medicine chest.

Meanwhile, unless the sufferer was under five or over sixty-five, there was nothing else to do, and no need to send a nurse ... if they could rustle up one, and they couldn't. It was useless, too, thinking of vaccines; the damage was done, also the 'flu had caught the country unprepared, there had been no pertinent preventative prepared yet.

'Just common sense, my dear,' Doctor Williams said in an asleep-on-his-feet tone. 'By any happy chance are you something of a nurse yourself?'

'Something only.'

'Then you are a nurse,' encouraged Doctor Williams, and rang off.

All that day, and the next, Paddy ran from flat to flat, tending, applying, changing soaked sheets, pressing cooling foments to brows, keeping warm, keeping cool, persuading to take sips and bites.

The third day she saw a change in the boys, but not, yet, Magnus. Magnus was still very ill. What made him worse was his continual worry. The stable, the horses, the blind mare and her foal . . . the white hope Into the Light.

'They're all right,' Paddy assured him.

'How do you know?'

'I've been there,' she lied . . . how many more lies? . . . 'and all the hands are in the pink. You're being done without very well, thank you.'

'Oh.' For the first time he looked a little better, and presently he slept, not tightly as before, heavily, but with easier and regular breathing, and a pinker look about him as he did so.

It was that burden off his mind, Paddy knew . . . and at once she knew the burden on hers. How did she know that the men in the stables were unaffected? It had been easy to tell the lie to Magnus, but what if they were shorthanded down there? What if——

The more she thought about it, Paddy knew she must find out. She looked at Magnus and saw that he would sleep for hours, looked in at the boys and saw that although they were improved they were still not up to the stage of moving, then quickly left the house.

The first thing that struck her was the quietness of the world outside the house. Usually there was a sound somewhere . . . a rattle of a bucket, a ring of a hoof as a horse was exercised, a clang, distant voices, laughter, men yarning.

It was a completely silent world.

Shivering a little, Paddy hurried across the field. She expected victims. An attack like this must strike some of them down, even though they were hard, tough, outdoor men, and never seemed to ail anything, but what greeted Paddy really shook her.

There was absolutely no one in attendance. There never were many, for the stud was run automatically, but there were several strappers, stablehands, exercise boys, and the resident caretaker was always here. These, with Richard and Paul, and, of course, Big Boss, had been enough. Now she could see no one.

She went from outbuilding to outbuilding without meeting one man, then ran ... for she was definitely alarmed now ... across to the caretaker's. His neat little cottage was unlocked, and Paddy walked in. There was no one there, and for an hysterical moment Paddy thought of the Marie Celeste ... then she saw the note on the table.

'Crook. Gone to Joe's.' Joe was the book-keeper. 'Sorry. Sam.'

Paddy put the letter down. That meant an entirely empty stud, and she had told Magnus——

She did a round of the stables. Everything seemed to be all right. The sick hands, before they had left, had prepared everything, and the fodder and water were mechanically controlled. But prize bloodstock needed more than that, Paddy fretted. They needed grooming, exercise, things that could not be done by automata.

She went across to blind Melisande's paddock. The mare was cropping peacefully, her ears as always on the alert for her child, for her ears had to act, too, for her sightless eyes.

'Dear Melisande,' Paddy fondled, 'you're all right,

anyhow, and so is your daughter, but what about your firstborn, the white hope? How is Into the Light?' She hurried across now to see.

There was no difference in Magnus's special boy, but Paddy was sensible enough to see that there could be. A carefully nurtured animal like this needed constant attention, and where was any constant attention? Where was any attention at all?

'I can't give it to you,' she told the acorn-coloured beauty forlornly, 'I've five of my own to attend to, and even if I had time I haven't the learning. That takes skill and know-how and——'

She stopped. She knew someone who did have skill and know-how, in fact even Magnus had spoken of him as the best trainer he had had: Kip.

She wondered if Kip, too, had succumbed. Not that it made any difference if he hadn't, of course, she still couldn't possibly, she would still never—Why, Magnus David would never forgive her.

Yet in a case like this ... Paddy looked at the lovely creature again in its well prepared, well planned but still restricted box.

At that moment Into the Light whinnied, and Paddy knew what had to be done. She went back to the house.

The boys had drifted off to sleep again, they looked brighter and much better, but they were still weak and still in need of bed. She checked Magnus. He slept very deeply now. She went out to the hall, switched through the phone to her own unit for privacy, then went and rang Standen Stud.

Rather to her surprise, for she had expected a delay while Kip was found, Kip answered himself.

'Norris here.'

'It's Paddy, Kip.'

'Padua, my dear!' he exclaimed.

'Kip, I'm concerned,' she told him.

'Not as concerned as I've been about you. I heard through the plateau grapevine that Yoothamurra went down badly with the bug.'

'Not I ... well, not yet.' Paddy added that because all at once she was feeling terribly tired. 'But,' she said, 'the rest.'

'By the rest you mean——?'

'All the hands, the boys——'

'David?'

'Yes.'

Kip whistled from the other end.

'Even Sam the caretaker had to give in,' she went on. 'Joe, the book-keeper, took him home with him.'

'Leaving the stud deserted?'

'Yes.'

Another whistle from the other end.

'I've been across, Kip, and so far things seem all right, but I know the attention that must be given, and it's not being given. Kip, what am I to do?'

'The answer's obvious, my dear, but unfortunately it can't be carried out.'

'What do you mean, Kip?'

'The answer is me, of course. A lot of them here have gone down, but not yours truly. Yes, I could come to your rescue, Padua, but on the other hand I couldn't, for obvious reasons I couldn't.'

'Why, Kip?'

'His Nibs. He would have a fatal relapse if he knew I'd lent a hand.'

'In a case like this?'

'Any case,' he assured her.

'But you told me you'd simply dissolved your employment with him, no bad words.'

'That's true,' he agreed, 'unless you count an order never to enter Yoothamurra Stud any more as a bad word.'

'Did he?'

'He did.'

'Oh!' Paddy stood wretchedly with the receiver in her hand, wondering what she could do. Blessedly, or so it came to Paddy, Kip came to her rescue.

'You said even Sam the caretaker is away?'

'*There's no one there at all.*'

'Then, Padua——'

'Yes?'

'I'll just have to come, won't I?'

'Oh, thank you, thank you, Kip!'

'There's only one thing. I don't wish to involve you.'

Paddy protested, 'But I'd have to be involved.'

'If I have to involve you,' Kip said firmly, 'I don't come. It's as basic as that. I know David and I know his vile temper. I won't have you suffer for having a kind heart.'

'But how otherwise?'

'Simple. You just know nothing about it.'

'But——'

'You naturally have the appropriate keys?'

'Why, yes.'

'Then leave them in the delivery box at the paddock gate. I'll pick them up, do what has to be done, put them back.'

'It's deceitful,' she sighed.

'That's the only commodity David deals in. Anyway,

please yourself, a small deceit or——?'

'You're right, of course. And Kip, you're so kind.'

'Just put those keys there now, pet, I'll see to the rest.'

'I wish I could repay you.'

'You will,' he assured her. 'Now do that little job, then get back to your patients, Nurse. Lucky patients!'

'Lucky me having a friend like you,' smiled Paddy.

'Lucky me having ... oh, we could keep this up for ever. Now off you go, love. And Padua——'

'Yes, Kip?'

'Worry no more. It's all in my hands. I'll see to everything, then put the keys back for you to pick up.'

'Thank you, Kip.'

'Thank *you*, darling.'

'For what? I've gone and given you a chore.'

'Thank you for turning to me,' Kip said smoothly. 'What else could a man ask?'

On that nice note it ended. Paddy put up the receiver, tiptoed into Magnus's room and removed the keys, then went out of the house and along to the delivery box at the road end of the stud buildings.

Kip was discreet. It was not until she was entering the house again that she saw him ride down the track and remove the keys. Even then he did not avail himself at once, he went back to Standen again, showing prudence, she thought. He evidently intended to wait until he was quite certain that no one ... meaning Magnus David ... was about.

She went to the transferred phone and rang Standen again. She told Kip she had seen him take the keys, but he need not have worried, Magnus David certainly would not be around today.

'Thank you, but I'll still do the necessary late this

afternoon. It should be super safe then. You'll find the keys put back.'

Paddy did find them in the box. She did not see Kip, though, and she mentally congratulated herself for doing things so adroitly.

Only once did she feel any alarm. As she was replacing the keys where Magnus had thrown them, the patient stirred and looked across at her. But he was too drowsy to look long. At once his eyes were closing again. He looked better, she thought. Possibly tomorrow, or the day after, he would be as fit as ever.

The boys meanwhile were very near to recovery. They were beginning to argue with each other, a sure sign.

But Paddy was feeling awful. Just as the boys got up and Magnus David sat up prior to getting up as well, she went down with her dose of virus.

Now she knew why Magnus, though he had worried about the stud, had been unable to stir himself. She was worried about the boys, and who would look after them, for Mrs Dermott had not recovered as quickly as she should, but still Paddy could not do anything about her concern.

She seemed riveted to her bed, and she knew even if she broke loose she would not be able to stand, her legs would not support her. Her head ached, her bones ached, all of her ached, everything seemed to be comprised of pain.

She was aware but uncaring of the boys peeping in at her, aware but still uncaring of Magnus David doing things for her that would ordinarily have sent her bounding out of bed to lock the door on him.

She was aware of tiptoeing, of things put down beside her, of arms around her supporting her while she drank and swallowed something, and if she didn't swallow it then held like that until she did. She was aware of all indignity, but she couldn't have cared less. Even when she heard Magnus David mutter one day: 'Why in tarnation is the phone switched in here?' did Paddy worry. She must have forgotten to switch it back after her talks with Kip, but who cared? Who cared?

She sweated, became chill again, tossed, went into deep sleep, then finally, a few days later, started to come out.

'All right,' invited Magnus David, sitting by her bed watching her, 'say it. Say where am I?'

'I know where I am.'

'Good for you—I didn't at first. What a bout! I've never had anything like it in my life. Had Jeremy been here he would have gone out like a match.'

'Yes.'

'But no one's gone out. All accounted for, and for that I have to thank you.'

'Me?' she questioned.

'You worked ceaselessly over us, you must have been run off your feet—no wonder you fell, too, in the end. But not only us, you attended the stud, something I'll never forget. When I went over and found that everyone had gone off but that everything was still as it needed to be, I—well, I was petrified. How did you do it, girl wonder?'

'Everything's automatic,' said Paddy feebly, 'I really mean it didn't entail much.'

'Not entail much, when I found Into the Light as spry as he ever was? And to think you did it! You groomed and rubbed and exercised him—how, a new raw rider, no experience, also just about ready to drop yourself, I'll never know.—Miss Travis, Miss Paddy Travis, how do you feel when I tell you that never, *never* have I known anyone less wanting?'

How did she feel? Paddy felt as low as she could have felt. She said: 'It's been awful. I want to forget it. Can't we drop it, please?'

'*I* will never drop it. But if you don't feel like talking about it now, then I'll go along with you. Some bad news, though, Mrs D. is still not able to come in. Do you think you can stand my cooking a little longer?'

'I don't know,' she smiled weakly, 'I've really tried very little of it.'

'No, and I'll come clean, it's not my cooking, I bring a prepared dish up from the stud. However, the boys are a hundred per cent again now, and assure me they can manage. I'm a great believer in that, so I think I'll go along with them and say yes. Meanwhile the stable cook has brewed barley broth. Will you take some?'

'Yes,' agreed Paddy rather apprehensively, for Magnus's announcement that the boys were taking over had not thrilled her. She had had experience of eager young cooks before, and she knew the strange results.

In the late afternoon she heard the noise of four boys in the kitchen arguing as to which switch to turn on and how far to turn it. Eventually a black chop arrived and four smiling faces. When Paddy managed to pierce the burnt offering, blood gushed out.

'We did it,' they announced.

Paddy ate it, and ate her omelette next morning ... Richard called it that and Paddy was glad, because otherwise she would not have recognised it ... but the following morning she had had enough. How could anyone frizzle the surrounds of an egg, she wondered, yet keep the middle raw? She determined as soon as the four left ... they were all back to normal activities now ... to get up. She had another reason for not dallying any longer. Mark, as he had brought in the remarkable egg, had said:

'We were looking through your banana cookbook.'

'Mr David's,' she corrected.

'There's a recipe for banana preserve. Have you ever heard of that?'

'No,' Paddy had said a little faintly.

'It's all right, except there's not much taste. So we put in a lot of salt and pepper.'

'Salt and pepper?' she gasped.

'But Richard likes sweet things, so we put in a lot of sugar, too.'

'Mark, you're having fun with me, of course?' But Mark had gone, leaving Paddy with the remarkable egg.

As soon as she heard the door bang, she got up. She swayed for a while, and then she found her feet. She tottered next door. On the table were filled jars and on the floor were contents that should have gone into jars but somehow had not reached there.

The colour of the jam-chutney-preserve, whatever it was, was horrific, something between smudge-blue and pollution-grey. Paddy approached the table and put out a testing finger. The concoction was watery but appeared also to be lumpy here and there. She tasted it and it was cane-sweet, yet seaweed-salt at the same time. Also, it burned. But most of all was its presence, all over stove, all over the table, all over the floor.

'What in tarnation——' Magnus David was standing at the door staring at the mess, and, forgetting she had come out in her nightie, Paddy defended:

'They did it to help me. You said they could.'

'I said they could cook, not concoct. What is it?'

'It's out of your mother's book.'

'Right out from now on. Which page?' Magnus had taken up the book from the table where it rested ... also covered with jam-chutney-preserve.

'No, don't do that,' said Paddy. 'They might have read it wrongly.'

'Well, they won't read me wrongly tonight. Little fiends!'

Paddy protested, 'They meant well.'

'They meant mischief. No one puts salt, sugar and pepper together like that and doesn't.'

'How do you know it's salt, sugar and pepper?'

'I just tried,' he groaned, and he looked across at Paddy and grimaced.

Then suddenly ... Paddy did not know who started it ... they were laughing, laughing hilariously. Magnus was helping her scour and rub and mop and dry, and she was stopping him from discarding the concoction.

'Because,' she pleaded, 'it meant something to them.'

'I'd like to make it mean a lot more—and by heaven I will! They can eat it for dinner tonight. But how well are you, Miss Travis?'

'You mean well enough to eat it, too?' she asked without enthusiasm.

'I mean well enough to eat out. To go out. Oh, I know you're just out of bed, but if we drive there and back——'

'Where?'

'The Plateau Club. There's a restaurant-cabaret there. Not bad, though I seldom go myself. Too much shop talk.'

'Then——' she began.

'But there won't be tonight.' All at once his eyes were flicking at her, not deriding as they always did, also not sympathising as he had when she had been laid low.

'What will there be tonight, then?' she heard herself ask.

'Soft music. Candlelight. Who knows? Hands across the table.'

A little wildly Paddy said: 'If you meant mine——'

'I did.'

'They'll have chutney under the nails.'

'Then we must see to that, mustn't we?' He was taking her to the bathroom, the boys' bathroom with the pick-aback soap. There he was cleaning each finger in turn, and suddenly it came to Paddy that it was a very enjoyable process having each nail examined, then meticulously cleansed.

But—the club? She bit her lip. Suppose Kip was there? Suppose he came across and said——

But Kip wouldn't, for it had been Kip who had been so adamant on her not telling Magnus.

'Seven,' Magnus was saying, drying the last finger. 'And until then, rest.'

'Seven?' she queried.

'I'll book a table for then.'

'But——'

She was in his big arms and he was carrying her into her own unit, putting her on the bed.

'Sleep, little one,' he said, and he pulled up the rugs and left her there.

Paddy heard him go out, but she still stayed where he had deposited her. She felt ... she didn't know how she felt ... except that it was nice.

CHAPTER NINE

PADDY rested obediently as instructed. Something inside her was urging her to look as good as she could tonight, and that would take complete relaxation now, for even getting up today had been a hard physical effort.

She found she was almost ridiculously excited about the prospect before her, and put it down to a previous dearth of social activity in her life. There had been the usual boy-friends at high school, but after that dates had been very rare. She had been too busy studying, and any men she met had been students too hard at it, too, leaving finally only Jerry at Pelican Beach, and to him she had been just Paddy, Old Man, Maryrose, and meals had been picnic variety on a rock, certainly not with someone on the other side of a table, soft music, candlelight, hands——

Paddy dismissed the hands.

Fortunately she had brought one long skirt with her. Where would a girl be, she smiled, without a long skirt? She decided, eyes still closed, to wear the least utilitarian of her blouses. That should get her past even his critical eyes.

The boys arrived home and she got up and superintended their dinner. Richard had brought up the meat from cold storage, and Paddy, remembering another episode, took the opportunity to explain to him about fillet and scrag.

'I thought Bingo enjoyed his meal that night,' grinned Richard when she had finished.

'Well, now you're wise about fibres of different cuts,

Richard.' Paddy served him a big plate.

'Where's yours?' They all wanted to know.

'Mr David is taking me to the club tonight.'

'Like that?'—Paddy wore jeans and tank top.

'No, I'm going to change.'

'Change now,' they urged eagerly, and Paddy smiled and went to her room. Poor kids, she thought, they want a bit of glamour, but they'll never get it out of me. She looked, dubiously now, confident no longer, down at her skirt.

But something had happened to the outfit. It had been a good enough skirt, as well cut a black velvet as she could have bought, but still ordinary. But now it looked quite wonderful. There was a beautiful jewelled belt on it, and on the blouse there was a matching pendant and bracelet.

Then she saw the note.

'I looked in to see if you had obeyed orders and found that you had laid out your gear. Please accept Aunt Mirabel's trinkets, if only to brighten the boys' hearts. M.D.'

'Oh, I will,' said Paddy eagerly.

She showered and dressed and where the blouse and skirt had looked neat enough, when the jewelled belt was clipped round, and the pendant and bracelet added, it was a different story.

'I look ... I look ...' Paddy beamed at herself, well pleased.

When Magnus tapped on the door and she opened the door and he saw her, he only glanced very briefly. But that brief glance missed nothing, Paddy sensed.

'Thank you for Aunt Mirabel's jewels,' she proffered.

'Semi-precious only, in fact local stuff—quite a lot of

beryl and lesser sapphire is found down our valleys, so you needn't be afraid of losing anything irreplaceable. Come now and slay the boys.'

The boys were satisfactorily 'slayed', their eyes were like saucers. They gave appropriate wolf whistles, and Richard even foresaw Paddy getting herself a feller.

'What are you talking about?' demanded Magnus. 'I'm her feller.'

'Are you, sir?'

'The one who escorts a lady is always her feller.' Magnus added cautiously: 'For the night, of course. Are you ready, Milady?'

Yes, Milady was ready, and she went down to his waiting car.

It was not far to the club, a small tasteful building set in a thicket of trees, surrounded by patios lit with coloured lights and just now sending out sweet music.

'Dancing music,' said Magnus. 'They like that sort up here.'

Paddy did, too, but she did not say so. It might sound as though she wanted to dance, and though she did, she was not going to tell him. Probably he didn't dance himself. He had said he did not socialize.

He had booked a table, a corner table near a palm, good to look out from but nicely concealed if anyone looked in.

'Considering the remoteness here,' Magnus said, 'the food is excellent. Shall I order?'

'Please.'

'Any preferences?'

'Yes. No jam-chutney-preserve.'

'I'll keep that in mind,' he promised, and he chose, then took up the wine list.

Paddy was surprised at the number of attractive young females present. She asked Magnus if they came up from the valley.

'Some,' he said, 'but a lot of them would be strappers from the different studs.'

'Girl strappers?'

'Why not?'

'You have none yourself,' she pointed out.

'That was Norris's idea, not mine. As a matter of fact if he had had his way he would have had nobody, he would have employed only himself. He was a hog for work, and I must admit he certainly got through it. I was deeply impressed at first, then puzzled ... and then I caught on.'

'Caught on?' she queried.

'Caught on why,' said Magnus cryptically.

'Why he didn't employ more? But surely that would be your prerogative.'

'It was his. When I delegate a job, I delegate it entirely. He just kept the staff to a bare minimum. So much so that I——'

'Caught on?'

'*You* are catching on,' Magnus said.

'Perhaps Ki—perhaps Mr Norris didn't want to employ women.'

'He didn't want to employ anyone.'

Paddy suggested, 'He could have been considering your purse.'

'He could.' But Magnus's lips were curled.

'Probably,' persisted Paddy, 'he's a male-male, a disliker of the female sex.'

'Does *that* look like it?' Magnus laughed sarcastically, and nodded towards the opposite corner. Feeling suddenly cold, Paddy pulled aside a palm leaf and recognised Kip across the room. He was surrounded by at least four pretty girls. That did not dismay Paddy, but the fact that he was here did. What, she thought, am I to say if he comes across, or waves, or nods, or greets me, what am I to explain to Magnus when Magnus thinks I don't even know him?

But she need not have worried. At that moment Kip looked up and across, saw her and did not show any interest.

Thank heaven! Paddy began to relax again.

It was a good meal. The wine was fine. The music was pleasing. Kip seemed to have left, so Paddy could breathe easily again, enjoy herself. She smiled across at Magnus.

'This is nice,' she appreciated.

'Thank you. It's nice bringing you. I never enjoyed the place before.'

'Now you are enjoying it?'

'Very much so, but you must tell me the moment you feel tired, you're barely out of bed, remember.'

'I'll tell you.' Paddy tried not to look wistfully at the dance floor. She adored dancing and would have liked nothing better than to have joined the small crowd on the polished square.

At that moment the orchestra broke off for a request through the mike to the owner of a certain car to re-move it because—Some reason was given, but Paddy did not hear it in the noise of Magnus scraping his chair as he got to his feet.

'Damn,' he said.

'Yours?' asked Paddy.

'Yes. I can't see how it's in the way, but if it has to be removed, it has to be, I expect. The trouble is I got the last bit of handy parking, now I'll have to park the thing a long way away. Will you be all right?'

'In here?'

'You can get picked up in other places than cities.'

'Of course I'll be all right,' Paddy assured him. 'I'll enjoy watching.'

She watched Magnus go ... and someone else must have been watching, too. Within seconds Kip Norris was standing at her side ... no, not standing, bowing.

'May I?' He smiled and nodded to the floor.

'Kip, I can't, you know I can't.'

'He'll be ten minutes at least. There's not a spot anywhere close.'

'How do you know? Kip, what have you done?'

'Put a message over the loudspeaker, that's all. For heaven's sake, get up, Padua, or people will start to stare at us.'

'Then they can stare,' she said. 'This is awful. You are awful.'

'All's fair in love and war, and that's what this is all about, love for you, and war for David, if he stands in my way.'

'He can't stand now, he's not here.'

'And won't be for a while.' With that Kip leaned forward and drew Paddy into his arms.

He was an excellent dancer. Paddy went carefully at first, then let herself go to the lilt and rhythm.

'You shouldn't have,' she said.

'I had to.'

'If he comes back——'

'Then you can tell him the club made all the ladies get up ... they do, you know ... and that you got me.'

'That's a lie,' she protested.

'Padua, you're already deep in lies. What's another?'

'But I don't want to be a liar, Kip, I never have been one.'

'But you haven't been in love before, either.'

'I'm not now.'

'Yes, you are. With me.'

He swayed her to the music, his lips not far from her ears. The lights went out and he stopped talking and kissed each ear instead.

The lights went on again, and, miraculously, she was back at her table, Kip was gone, and——

And Magnus sat waiting for her.

Paddy sat down as well.

'The car,' he said, 'is round the other side.'

'Then shall we go?' she asked.

'Oh, no, not without a dance.'

'I ... you ...' she began.

'You think I don't dance? But I do. If I'd been here when the Ladies' Choice was on ... I believe they call them that ... you could have asked me, not Norris.'

'I—I had to get up.' There, the lie had started.

'Dear child, of course. And of all people you chanced on Kip Norris, my ex-trainer. I've already told you about Norris, remember? You said you two hadn't met.'

She nodded.

'But you have now. What did you talk about while you danced?'

'He's a very good dancer, quite an intricate one, I'm afraid it took me all my time to keep up with him.'

'Really? Then let's see how you go with me.'

If Paddy had thought Kip quick, then this man was wildfire. Barely had he spoken than she was on the floor with him, and they were dancing, and Paddy knew that prior to this dance she never had danced before.

One of his hands held one of her hands, and though the touch was featherlight at the same time it seemed made of steel. His other hand round her waist was almost impersonal, and yet it imprisoned her for all its deliberate slackness, it held her more tightly than she had ever been held in her life.

The band, as though sensing something, had quickened their strains, so perforce their steps quickened. And, like it or not, and she did like it, Paddy's blood quickened.

'What did he say to you?' Magnus was demanding.

'Who?'

'Norris.'

'Nothing.'

'Are you still sure you hadn't met him before?'

'I hadn't,' she insisted. 'I told you.'

'But you tell me a lot of lies, don't you? You deal in lies. "Remember September", that was a lie.'

'It's September now,' Paddy said a little stupidly.

'Yes, and it's a September, my God, that you *will* remember, not like poor Jeremy's spring.' Now Magnus made no pretence of impersonality, of indifference, he pulled her close to him and forced her to dance cheek by cheek. Round the floor they went, couples making way for them, dancers drifting off so they could have the small space to themselves, then standing and watching them.

Breath-close ... closer than Kip had been ... then deliberately Magnus David was putting his lips not to her ears, as Kip had done, but to her hair. Then, after her hair, her mouth.

'Tonight you are not found wanting,' he said.

The music stopped and they walked back to their

corner. Instinctively Paddy did not sit down, and she was right about that, for he said:

'We'll go now.'

They drove back in silence, and they entered the house in silence. When Paddy went through the door that led to her suite, she said: 'Goodnight.'

'Goodnight,' he said back.

Nothing more.

Paddy fumbled out of her clothes. She did not even replace the jewelled belt, pendant and bracelet as they deserved, she simply spilled them down with the rest of her gear, put out the light and slipped into bed.

She was shivering. The night was balmy, but she was still cold. After all that whirling round, she was still cold. After that kiss, she was still icy.

Because, she knew, he was only taunting me, Magnus David will always only be taunting me, and I don't want it like that, I want ... why, I want ...

She turned her head into her pillow, not believing her tumbling thoughts, not permitting them for one moment, trying to smile over them ...

The next morning she found she could.

Paddy coped with the meals for a few days, delighting the boys, who like all boys had a sweet tooth, with selections from Magnus David's mother's banana cookbook.

Brandy Banana Flambé was their favourite, but because of their years, and also because of no brandy, Paddy substituted caramel for the cognac. They were so enthusiastic they must have told Magnus about it, and he came into the kitchen and asked her: 'What's all this about Brandy Banana Flambé?'

'I took it from your banana cookbook.'

'But you didn't take any brandy from my bar, I've checked and the bottle's intact. Have you a secret source?'

'Oh, no, I use caramel instead.'

'For a Brandy Flambé?'

'Of course. Remember they're boys of tender years.'

'Tender? My God!' he said.

He left her but a few minutes later returned with a bottle of brandy.

'Make it again,' he ordered.

'But the boys——'

'I don't think it will set them on an alcoholic path,' she said. 'Besides, *I* want it, and I want Brandy, not Caramel Flambé.'

'Yes, sir,' agreed Paddy dubiously, 'though do you really think——'

'The boys?'

'Yes.'

'I do. You see, they'll be maturing a lot more in a short time.' She looked at him in puzzlement, and he explained: 'Little Lulu.'

'Oh, she's having her foal.'

'I hope. It's soon about to begin, I should say, but being Lulu——'

'And how will the event mature them?'

'I've spoken to them and they all want to be there.'

'Do you think that's wise?'

'I think it's very wise. I think it's even essential. By the way, *you* know all about birds and bees, of course?'

'Oh, don't be silly! she snapped. 'I'm twenty-one.'

'Meaning nothing.'

'Then don't forget' ... she could not stop herself

saying it, for every time he had spoken in the same strain to her she had hated him for it ... 'I had a month at Pelican Beach.'

He looked at her furiously, was obviously about to say something furious, then he stopped himself. Instead, after a moment, he admitted: 'I suppose I've asked for that.'

'And now you're asking for Brandy Banana Flambé.' She decided to accept his apology.

'Please.'

He watched her while she choose six large firm bananas, while she stirred cream into the cognac.

'I'm drooling already!' he grinned.

'I hope it will be all right,' said Paddy. 'I've only tried the boys' variety.'

'The boys will be men this week. Now don't ask me if it's wise again.'

'I won't.'

'You also didn't answer my question.'

'About?' she queried.

'About what you know or don't know.'

'I know what every girl should know,' she replied. 'Satisfied?'

'My question really was leading up to whether you had participated in a birth.'

'I'm childless,' she answered him with maddening misunderstanding. As he looked annoyed, she added hastily: 'No, I haven't. We were supposed to in the course, but we never actually got round to it.'

'Then you, too, must come.'

'Come where?'

'To the accouchement.'

'Why? I have no need to be separated between the boys and the men.'

'But you have between the girls and the women. You're not a woman yet, you're a damn cantankerous child.'

'I want to be co-operative,' said Paddy, 'but I can't see how watching Little Lulu will help.'

'You'll come, though. That's an order. You can send in one of the boys with a portion of the Brandy Flambé at dinner. I've work to do now.'

'Then don't let me keep you.'

He walked to the door, then turned.

'Do you think you could?' he asked.

Over the meal that night, Magnus's slice having been duly despatched, the boys were more excited over the imminent birth than they were over their sweet. In fact they ate it up without noticing any difference. All they could think of was Little Lulu.

'Horses take a long time,' announced Richard. 'They take eleven months. As Magnus told us, horses take longer even than you.'

'Me?' came in Paddy indignantly. Really, he was going too far!

'He actually said female humans,' came in Mark. 'You're that.'

'Elephants take longer still,' observed Paul.

'Are you all agreed you want to watch?' Paddy inquired.

'Oh, yes. Magnus said Little Lulu will like our concern. He's hoping she's quicker than last time. That was eight nights altogether.'

'But that was her first,' John reminded him.

'Seconds are shorter. It might be over quick-smart.'

They kept chattering on, curious, eager, all hopeful they could play a helpful part except Richard, *who knew, of course, he could*. Richard was like that.

'I'm a natural,' he boasted. 'I think I could even manage it all on my own.'

'No, Little Lulu,' said Paddy feelingly, 'will be doing that.'

Lulu was fooling in the western paddock, a favourite paddock with her; John told Paddy that Magnus had said she must favour its grass.

They had barely finished dinner when the summons came. They all trooped out ... Richard first, eager to prove that he was the man for the job. As they came up to the western paddock, now bright with lanterns, Magnus detached himself from a group of men and walked across.

'She's going fine, she won't take long this time. Our only worry is her impatient child, the brat is already fighting to enter the world, but Little Lulu is a more refined type of girl, not used to being pushed about like that. Look, boys, she's getting restless, and that's a sign. Contractions come next, and very soon the baby's two forelegs will appear.'

Even as Magnus said it, it was all happening. After the little forelegs came the head, a sweet, wet, very surprised head. Then all of Little Lulu's foal was born.

'A lovely boy,' triumphed Magnus. 'Now you four are five.' He grinned at them, then raised his brows. 'No, still four, I see, one of our party is missing.'

'Richard,' the three present chorused, 'he scrammed.'

'But Richard is the mastermind, isn't he?' Again Magnus grinned. 'Well, I told you' ... to Paddy now ... 'it sorted out the boys.—What about the women and the girls?'

But Paddy could not answer him. She was on her knees

beside the little newborn fellow, she was helping the attendant to tie the navel string.

She finished and looked up, looked up at Magnus, and in her eyes was all the tenderness in the world, all the love and warmth. Magnus David looked back, then he smiled deeply at her.

'You've been sorted, Paddy Travis,' he told her, then he turned quickly away and tried to get something out of his eye.

Richard joined them, angry with himself but still of the same opinion.

'I'm never going to be a mother,' he declared.

'You couldn't be if you wanted to, that's for girls.'

'I wouldn't anyway, and neither will my wife.'

'By that time,' cheered Magnus, 'they'll probably be issued gift-wrapped.'

Paddy listened to the chatter but did not really hear it. She felt deeply satisfied. She felt like Mother Earth. When they got back to the house and Magnus asked her to come to his flat to toast the newborn with him, she went, still in her wonderful daze.

'To Lulu's boy,' Magnus said after he had filled two glasses.

'To Lulu's boy.'

They drank, and when they had finished Paddy said goodnight to him, *still* in her Mother Earth aura.

It was not until she reached her room that she realised that before he had opened the door for her, he had kissed her, that she had kissed him back.

That it had not been that taunting kiss as at the club.

That it had been . . . fulfilment. As deep as life itself.

CHAPTER TEN

MRS DERMOTT, back to health, started fetching her dinner dishes ready to be heated for the evening meal again. She was a good cook, and the boys appreciated that, but they still made Paddy promise to slip in her own exciting Flambé now and then.

A letter had come from Closer Families with a guardian questionnaire to be filled in. It was a routine inquiry, and Paddy told Magnus David this as she stood beside him, pen waiting, while he scowled over her interrogation.

'They always want to know how the wards are faring,' she said.

'Can't you answer it yourself? You have eyes.'

'But I have to ask *you*. You are the sponsor, I'm only the house-mother.'

'Then yes, yes, yes, yes, yes.'

'Some questions might need No,' Paddy pointed out.

'I leave it to you.'

'Mr David, it is necessary that I——'

'But not necessary for me. You see, they're not going to be my wards ... oh, I know they are at present ... but—— well, they won't be.'

'You're relinquishing them?' Paddy's voice was shocked.

'They're becoming my sons.'

'The whole four?' she gasped.

'I don't intend picking and choosing, if that's what you mean.'

'It's a large family.'

'It will be larger when I have my own,' Magnus assured him.

'So you're getting married?'

'Yes.'

'Congratulations,' she said in a quiet voice.

'Thank you. Now where were you up to?'

'Yes, yes, yes, yes, and yes—— But, Mr David——' He raised his brows. 'Are you sure about these boys?'

'Applying to adopt them?'

'Applying for them with an image in view ... which you are. Richard, for instance, you thought you had a stud man in him, and he took one look at Little Lulu and raced off. But perhaps you've gained on the banana side. Yes, that would be it.'

'That would be what?'

'The cause for your satisfied expression.'

'Please tell me, Miss Travis,' said Magnus, 'what actually is a satisfied expression?'

'The expression you're wearing now, everything going your way.'

'Frankly, it is, but not as you think. Richard did have a change of mind about that side of the business, but has now embraced the commercial angle. He wants to be the accountant of Yoothamurra, not just the bookkeeper, and believe me, every stud needs a skilled money man. I think you'll find him *very* attentive at lessons.'

'Good for him, good for the stud, but not so good for your banana farm.'

'I'm not worried, I have a strong feeling my own children will be interested in that.'

'I thought you said these were to be your children.'

'They will.'

'But not "my own"?'

'Sharp, as always,' he drawled. 'Yes, they will be. I should have said my children and my wife's.'

'You first, of course.'

'Of course,' he agreed.

Paddy turned back to the form, wrote what was required and got Magnus to sign it.

'Thank you,' she said, and left him. She was a little piqued when he made no attempt to delay her.

Life resumed its old pattern. Paddy ate with the boys at morning and night, superintended their lessons, tidied the bathroom when they had left, left the rec room strictly as it was as such rooms with children working in them should be left ... did little else.

She seldom saw Magnus. There was a lot of activity going on in the stables, and the boss had to be there constantly, so Richard informed her. He added in confidence that they were beginning to put Into the Light through his paces. He spoke it in a voice of thrall.

Paddy would dearly have loved to have gone across, but not being asked she stayed at home. She did, anyway, until one exceptionally lovely morning, when she walked the track again and met Kip.

He emerged as he had before, almost as though he had been waiting for her.

'I haven't seen you since the club,' he complained, 'have you been avoiding me?'

'Of course not.'

'Then has he forbidden you? It's the sort of thing he'd do, for no doubt he soon found out who arranged that false message.'

'Mr David knows better than to forbid me,' said Paddy ... though not so sure herself.

'Good for you ... but not so good for me. I get so fed

up not seeing you, Padua, when *can* I see you? What do you do during the day?'

'Nothing really after the boys go until evening. That' ... a little laugh ... 'is why I'm here now.'

'Then what's to stop us having a day together? I'm off duty at that time, too. Padua, let's go down to the valley. I don't know if you've heard about it, but these valleys are full of gems, semi-precious stuff admittedly, but very pretty, and simply waiting to be washed out of the streams and creeks. There's grass stones, beryls, even sapphires of a sort.'

'Yes, I had heard, but——' Paddy was thinking of Magnus and how he would take it.

'But what?'

'But should I go?'

'On your own time off?'

'That's right, on my own time off,' agreed Paddy a little indignantly. After all, Magnus David did not rule her. 'Yes, I'd like to go with you, Kip. When?'

'Tomorrow. Same time.'

'Lovely. Do I ride or what?'

'You just come here as you did today, then we go down as far as we can in the four-wheel drive, then walk the rest. You'll love it.'

'I'm sure I will,' Paddy said.

She left at the same time the next morning. It had rained through the night, it rained often at nights up here, banana country had to have rain, and Paddy supposed that studs did not mind it. It made the air crystal clear the next day, the sky sapphire. Would that be a lucky omen now, she asked Kip when she met him, would she find a sapphire?

'I can't promise you anything, really, gems never jump

out at you, they have to be tracked down.' He showed her a pan he had brought. 'We'll fill it with silt, then grub,' he grinned.

They had a perfect morning, no sapphire, but certainly some gold specks, some rhodinite and blue agate. Paddy was entranced.

Pausing for a break for their aching backs, she found, without silting and grubbing, a lovely gem which Kip told her was the grass stone, properly called rutilated quartz, and of no commercial value. 'The only thing you can say,' he shrugged, 'is that it's found only in Australia and Chile.'

'It's beautiful,' she smiled.

'It is if you say so, Padua.'

'I do say so.'

'Then give it to me,' he said.

'Why?'

'Because I'm going to slip it on your finger ... don't worry, I'll hold it there, not drop it ... and then we're engaged.'

'Oh, Kip, you fool!'

'I'm serious,' he said. 'I've fallen for you, Padua.'

'Going by the number of girls around you the other night you often fall,' she said dryly.

'Yes, but this time, as the old musical comedy goes, I've got my foot caught in the door. I love you, Padua.'

The sun through the trees turned his fair hair to gold, he looked very handsome, very much the Greek god. Paddy was flattered.

'I'm taking this grass stone,' he said, 'and having it polished then set. Inside I will have inscribed: "Padua, A toi." '

'With Padua, it should be in Italian,' she commented.

'Whatever it's in, it comes down to the same. I do love you, my dear.'

They sat in the sweet cool bush. The creek where they had been panning accelerated its pace further down the valley and started a thousand waterbells. Kip had put the stone away in his pocket and was now playing with another object.

'What's that?' Paddy asked.

'A stopwatch. Surely you've seen a stopwatch before?'

'I guess so, but I've never looked at one properly.'

'Look at this one now.' He handed it over, then proceeded to tell her how to work with it.

'Take that bit of floating bark up there,' he indicated when he thought she had grasped the idea.

'There?' She pointed.

'Yes. Now time it to that clump of ferns.'

Paddy did so and triumphantly gave her result.

'You're a wizard. Right, first go.—Keep it, Padua.'

'Keep it? But——'

'I have as many stopwatches as I have socks,' he shrugged. 'Trainers do.'

'It's nice of you, Kip, but what do I want with it?'

'You could find it handy. You could time those kids of yours as to how long they take to the school bus ... Or'—the slightest of pauses—'you could time some of the horses. Into the Light, for instance, when he's being tried out. That should be very interesting.'

'Yes,' said Paddy, feeling oddly uneasy for some reason.

'Only I wouldn't advise you to do it with him about, he's an odd cuss.'

'Magnus?' she asked.

'Who else? But what can you expect with a name like that?'

'You have an unusual name yourself, Kip. Is it a nickname?'

'No.' He grimaced and shrugged.

'Short for Kipling?'

'Yes. My mother was keen on poetry and Kipling was her favourite poet. Thank heaven I took after my father, he had a mathematical brain. Poetry doesn't feed you but figures do.'

'So prosaic. I, too, love Kipling. And I thought you would have, Kip. Kipling was very much the man.'

'So am I,' said Kip, and he drew her close.

When she returned to the house in the afternoon, Magnus David was there. She hadn't seen him all the week and he startled her with his sudden appearance. She had walked back slowly, savouring the day, and ... yes, savouring the thought of Kip. So handsome and so in love with her. It was a nice feeling to have someone so nice as Kip in love with you. Paddy felt for and took out the stopwatch. How absurd he was giving her this!

'Miss Travis!'

Paddy actually jumped and only kept the stopwatch in her hand by a distinct effort.

'What on earth are you carrying round?' he asked irritably. 'A bird's nest? Or have you struck gold?'

'Neither.'

'That I can't believe, you have something jealously locked away in those clenched hands.'

'Nothing,' she insisted.

'I could open them, you know.'

'As boss you can do anything,' she agreed too smoothly.

'I thought not seeing you for a while might have improved you, but it hasn't.' He stepped back for her to pass him.

'Did you want me?' she asked.

'No.'

'But you said my name.'

'I just wanted to see if you still answered to it.'

'You're being ridiculous!'

'No, factual. You could have been married during this last week.'

'I was not married,' she shrugged.

'Nor engaged?'

At once Paddy thought of the grass stone that had been held to her appropriate finger, that Kip had taken with him to be set ... then inscribed.

'No.' But she did not say it promptly, and he noticed that.

'So!' he said.

'Is that all?'

'Certainly. Take yourself ... and your bird's nest or egg or what-have-you ... into your own unit.'

'Yes, sir.' Paddy went.

But when she got to her room she unclenched the stop-watch with distaste. Stupid thing, it could have got her into trouble. She found a handkerchief and wrapped it loosely in it and put it in a drawer.

The next day Magnus appeared to have forgotten the episode. He called in after the boys and Mrs Dermott had left.

'Ever been to the races?' he asked.

'No.'

'Then you're going now.'

'Where?'

'Oh, nothing grand, just some picnic races. As a matter of fact I'm giving Into the Light his first try. I'm not expecting anything, and I'm certainly not pushing for anything. It will be a pleasant outing, and I think you'll like it. Can you be ready in half an hour?'

'Oh, yes,' said Paddy eagerly. She had never attended any kind of race meeting, country, picnic or big stuff, and was excited.

She hurried to her room, stood a moment considering the subject of dress, then took out a faithful shirtwaister. Shirtwaisters were trim and neat and generally acceptable anywhere, she thought.

She brushed her hair ... not far from the colour of Into the Light's acorn ... put on a very pink lipstick and that was that.

When she came out Magnus said: 'It's good to see one girl instead of five boys for a change.' She knew he meant her skirts. She always wore jeans around the house.

He paused, rummaged in his pocket, then brought out some banknotes and gave them to her.

'What's this for?'

'What do you think?'

'To get in?'

'No, I'm a member, of course. But you don't go to races and just look into distance, Miss Travis.'

'Oh, but I want to look,' she insisted. 'I'll be most interested.'

'You'll be expected to be more than interested, you'll be expected to participate. The bookies who fly up only do so in the assurance that it will be worth their while.'

'You mean—bet with this?'

'You're catching on!' he drawled.

Paddy asked, 'Shall I put it all on Into the Light?'

'No, I don't recommend that, unless you place him. The feller's not quite ready yet. Now if you're ready——'

'Oh, I am!'

The small racecourse was on the plateau. There was also a larger one, Magnus said, for the annual Cup and Plate. It must be a bigger plateau than she had thought, Paddy remarked as they drove along, to boast two.

'Big enough,' he agreed. 'Four valleys reach up here and form a fair-sized table top. Here's the minor course now, nothing elaborate, but quite pleasing. You'll see a lot of faces you saw at the club.' He broke off sharply, and Paddy knew he was thinking, as she was, of Kip Norris.

They entered, and Magnus found the members' special parking section for his car.

'I'll go round and check up on our boy,' he said. 'You can mooch around, find something to stop you from being bored, have a bite in the tea tent before the crowd begins. Events don't start for an hour.'

Magnus need not have worried about the bored bit, Paddy smiled later; she had never been more entertained in her life.

She passed through a row of bookmakers' stands and had a wager on something called Fiddlesticks because the name amused her. Then she settled herself by the parade ring and enjoyed the silks and satins and glowing colours, but most of all the shining horses.

She decided on tea before all the tables were taken. After that she heard the warning for the first race. It was all wonderful and she would not have missed it for the world. The attendance, though comparatively small when you considered city meetings, let out a deep-throated roar as the horses went by.

'Why, I've won!' Paddy laughed.

Somebody laughed with her. Kip did.

'It's all right,' he said at her look of concern, 'we're

as concealed in this push as we would be in the middle of a maze. What brought you here?'

'Who,' she corrected. 'Mr David.'

'Oh. Where is he?'

'In Into the Light's box.'

'Yes, the boyo's entered for the Sun Up, isn't he? It's not an important race, I mean no big stakes, but it's considered a forerunner of the Plate, and that really is something. Good prizes, and an influx from Sydney. Staged at the big ring, incidentally. I suppose this is more or less a tryout for the white hope?'

'Yes ... I suppose it is.'

'How's he been doing?' asked Kip.

'I don't know.'

'Don't know? What did I give you a stopwatch for? There' ... at a look on Paddy's face ... 'I'm joking, of course. But you must have some idea. For instance, did David have a pleased look or not?'

'Just the same look.'

'Did he tell you anything?'

'Like what?' she queried.

'Like whether to back him or not. I know you're betting, because you just won.'

'Kip, why are you so interested?' she asked.

'Darling, I'd just like to win myself some pocket-money, the same as you.'

'Of course,' Paddy agreed. 'For a moment I thought——'

'Yes?'

'That you were interested in more than that.'

'Not me. And yet in a way that's untrue. I'd like to get enough money to have a stable of my own, not manage it for someone else. Somewhere away from here, but' ... taking her hand ... 'never away from you.'

'But I love this place.'

'I love *you*, and whither I go you should come.'

'Kip, you're the very end!' Paddy had to laugh. 'You don't, you simply don't, say things like that at races.'

'I do and I have. Well, what did His Nibs advise regarding Into the Light for the Sun Up?'

'A place only.'

'Good. Go ahead and do it, then come back here.'

'Is it—I mean——'

'Is it safe?' he interpreted. That had been the word she had wanted, but she had felt cheap using it. 'Of course it's safe, Miss Caution. Always pick a crowd. Now hurry away, then hurry back, I want to show you all the finer points of racing.'

But it was Magnus who did that, not Kip. Magnus met her as she was crossing the courtyard, and he got into step beside her, evidently intending to spend the rest of the day instructing her. There was no chance of alerting Kip, but Kip, Paddy half-smiled, would never need alerting. She did not see him for the rest of the afternoon.

Standing by the rails Paddy heard herself cheering Into the Light from the rear, where he found himself, to third place. When there was a bunch-up once she cried out in dismay, but when he moved up on the inside and Magnus told her there were only five furlongs to go, she shouted with the rest. She only stopped when it was all over and Magnus stood grinning down at her.

'Well, House-mother,' he laughed, 'a little bit different from Brandy Flambé, isn't it? Let's get your winnings and hit home before the crowd. It mightn't be a Melbourne Cup crowd, but after all, we've only one road.'

He was a different Magnus all the way back. He teased her, he recommended all sorts of extravagant things to buy with her small winnings, he was . . . he was even boyish.

They parted on a happy note, which made the next meeting, exactly five minutes afterwards, all the bigger shock.

Paddy had only put her things down, had not even changed out of her dress. She had stood wondering a moment at the drawer in her cupboard, she had not remembered leaving it open.

But she had little time to wonder. Without any warning and certainly no knock, Magnus came striding in.

'What's the explanation of this?' he demanded.

She stood without comprehension for quite a while, then her glance dropped to what he held out at her. It had been Kip's, but now it was hers. It was the stopwatch.

'It's a stopwatch,' she said dully.

'I know what it is, but I want the explanation. For instance, how do you happen to have it? Why?'

But Paddy was puzzling why *he* had it. She had wrapped it up in a handkerchief, put it in a drawer, she was sure she had.—A drawer?

Now she was remembering. Just as she was leaving, Richard had come from the stud with the request of all humble things of a safety pin.

'A safety pin?' she had said, 'but surely you'd have one.' Then she had recalled his sex, a sex more given to rivets and valves poked into pockets, and had tossed:

'Look for yourself, dear. It'll be in one of my drawers.'

Whether he had found the safety pin she did not know, but he had found a stopwatch. He shouldn't have

132

taken it, but probably he'd only borrowed it to try out something, a boy would do that. And now Magnus had seen him.

'Richard?' she asked.

'Yes. He was bringing it back, and I must say he didn't carry it as secretively as you carried that bird's egg.' Magnus laughed without mirth. 'All right, I'm waiting.'

'It's nothing, of course,' Paddy began. 'We all get these stopwatches.'

'You surprise me. Tell me more. Do you time the kids' waking up?'

'No, but Closer Families had this outdoor physical activity thing as well as its other functions. Some of us' ... Paddy drew a breath ... 'were interested in athletics and bought ourselves these watches.'

'You said before you got them.'

'Yes. At a sports shop.'

'And when you did, you bought the very best,' he said drily. He handed the stopwatch across.

'You don't believe me, do you?' How could she, *how could she*, Paddy thought, keep lying like this?

'Short of ringing up Mr Aston, which I won't do, I'll have to, won't I? No, I'll believe you, but' ... a flick of his eyes ... 'many wouldn't.'

He turned on his heel without another word, and Paddy finished changing her clothes.

The fun had gone, the excitement had gone, and she wished very much that the stopwatch had gone. Perhaps if she left it around ... But no, that was an important lesson in the Manual. Never put temptation on display.

It's my fault, she knew, I never should have accepted it, or if I did I should have been honest about it. How many lies have I told now? What did Kip say?

'Padua, you're already deep in lies. What's another?'

But to me, Paddy thought miserably, this one is just the last straw. Where is the girl who ran along the sands with Jerry at Pelican Beach one long September ago?

It's September again now, a September Jerry's brother said to me: 'My God, you *will* remember.' And though I don't blame him, not in this web I've spun, I still wish he'd forget, and that I'd never started to deceive.

CHAPTER ELEVEN

THERE was a subtle difference in Magnus after that. He was neither openly critical nor frankly antagonistic any more, instead he controlled, if thinly, his undoubted dislike of her. Also, he was withdrawn.

He was something else as well, something Paddy found very distasteful. He was watchful—she felt sure of it. Watchful of whom? It would have to be her, of course, but why? And watchful for what reason?

It all made no sense, but it did make Paddy very miserable. Rightly or wrongly she became obsessed with the stopwatch. She entirely blamed the stopwatch. Before the stopwatch affair he hadn't been like this. He had been an enemy, yes, but occasionally a tolerant one. Now——

She would simply have to return the thing to Kip, make him take it. If he wouldn't, she would throw it away. The existence of the wretched instrument was getting her down. She could have gladly put it on the floor and jumped on it.

She looked for an opportunity to take a walk again in the Standen Stud vicinity, but always Magnus seemed to appear just as she was about to leave. She almost began to think of herself as a prisoner.

Then Magnus announced one evening that he was going down to Sydney. He said it in that unrevealing way he had adopted of late.

'On important business, extremely important to me.'

'I know it,' Paddy heard herself saying piteously to him, 'it's the wretched stopwatch. You're going to ask Mr Aston if I was telling the truth when I said it was advised that we equip ourselves with them. Very well then, Mr David, I now intend to——'

Actually she had been about to say, 'I now intend to tell you the truth,' even at the risk of his wrath, for she knew he would be very angry.

But she never got that far. He looked at her in surprise, then said: 'You *are* obsessed, aren't you? Do you always take a reprimand to heart like that? Good heavens, weren't you ever spanked?'

'Yes—by you. Over that watch.'

'My dear child, *that* was only a tap. When I do find cause to punish you ...' he laughed.

Except that she was so relieved that she was on the wrong course, Paddy would have picked him up over that '... when I do find cause to punish you.'

'Then—then what are you going for?' she asked thankfully.

'It's none of your business, but I'll still tell you. This house ... castle, you call it .... is extremely old. No doubt you've noticed that.'

'Old and beautiful.'

'I agree, and evidently others agree as well. I think I

told you once the National Trust was interested.'

'Yes, when I first came here.'

'They've been in touch again, and they want to take it over.'

'Would you like that?' she asked.

'I would be proud of that. As it is now, with three distinct units, it's not its gracious self.'

Paddy asked, 'Where would you live?'

'In the plantation house, of course—much more to my liking for a family home.'

'But you're not a family, are you?'

'I will be when I legally adopt the boys.'

'Or when you marry and have more boys.'

'A girl or two would be allowed,' he drawled. 'Regarding the wards,' he went on, 'the slow and deliberate way adoption moves, they'll probably be living in their own quarters before it's through.' He jerked his head towards the window and beyond the window to the cluster of buildings. 'They're all still keen on bloodstock, and that includes Richard, Little Lulu's confinement and all.'

'You would live at your work, too?'

'I told you, I would live with my family in the banana house. It's not far to travel each day. Now don't say there's no family, because there will be.' He caught and held her eyes. He held them for so long that she had to turn away.

'I'll be gone a week,' he said.

There was no reason now for Paddy to sneak out, and on the first morning she walked quite openly to Standen, and even, when Kip came out, accepted his invitation to look the place over.

It was as big and as well equipped as Yoothamurra;

Magnus had told her that there were only the two big studs, that the rest only dabbled.

Kip took her everywhere, even places where Paddy might have stood back, fearing she could be intruding.

'Don't worry,' Kip assured her, 'old Standen's in England. I'm in complete control. My God, if I only were *always*! That's what I want, Padua, that's what I must have. I have the ability, in fact I have exceptional ability.'

'Yes, Mr David said that,' she agreed.

'But he's never tried to get me back, has he?' Kip said it more to himself.

He looked brooding, so Paddy tried to brighten him with an airy: 'So your boss is away? So is mine.'

'David's away?'

'Yes.' She told him the reason ... well, that shouldn't be secret, if he didn't know he'd know when the National Trust stepped in.

'Fool,' said Kip. 'I wouldn't do any handing over, I'd get good hard cash.'

'But Kip, Yoothamurra is beautiful.'

'So is money. I'm sorry, sweetheart, but you simply have to have money.'

'Yes,' nodded Paddy with gentle bemusement, 'I see now why you shouldn't have been called after a poet.'

'But you still love me?'

She hesitated at that. He was physically all a girl could ask, and he was gallant and very much the eager lover, but——

Fortunately he was not attending.

'How long will he be away?' he asked.

'A week.'

'Could be better, could be worse.'

'What do you mean, Kip?'

'Little greenhorn!' He kissed her. 'See this fellow' ...
her drew her along to a box and introduced a splendid
stallion ... 'he's Standen's answer to your nag.'

'Don't call him that!'

'Son of Darkness ... oh, I remember, it's Into the Light.
Forgive me, sweetheart.'

When he looked like that at her, Paddy would have
forgiven him anything. She touched the silk of the magnificent horse.

'Name?' she asked.

'Peerless Prince.'

'He looks every inch of it.'

'He'll prove it.' A long quizzical look at Paddy 'You
could help, you know.'

'Help?'

'And why shouldn't you? Every woman should help
her man, and I am your man, aren't I, Padua?'

'How could I help?' she asked.

'I gave you a stopwatch.'

'Which I'm returning right now.' She took it out and
handed it to him. 'That's really what I came for, Kip.'

'To return the watch?'

'Yes.'

'But you know how to use it. I thought you caught
on very quickly.'

'But I didn't want it. You pushed it on me. What in
heaven would I do with a stopwatch?'

Kip said carefully : 'Time a few nags—I mean time a
few boyos for me.' At a look on her face he said quickly :
'There's nothing wrong with that, everyone does it. In
Sydney or Melbourne the timing crowd at the rails in
the week before a big race is almost as large as when the
race is run. It's perfectly legitimate, you goose.'

'Then why don't you——'

'Because I'm not allowed in, that's why. You are. You belong there.'

'But I couldn't time a horse.'

'Perhaps not openly, I agree a character like David wouldn't care about that. But you could still do it secretly—just happen to be passing by, that kind of thing. You'd be the last person in the world he'd suspect of doing a thing like that.'

'You're wrong,' said Paddy, 'I'd be the first.'

'What?'

'I'd be the first he'd suspect. You see, he found out I had this thing and——' But she could not go on. All at once Kip's face was close to hers, and it wasn't a pleasant face any more.

'You damn little fool to let him find out!' He fairly gritted it.

'I couldn't help it,' she protested.

'Of course you could help it. Oh, lor', preserve me from sweet innocents from this day on! What did he say? What did he suspect?'

'Suspect?'

'Suspect of you—and someone else?'

'I don't understand you,' said Paddy.

'Then that makes two of us. *I* can't understand such utter imbecility.'

'Kip, you're being unfair. It was all out of my hands, and anyway, it turned out all right. I told him it was a Closer Families issue for the phys. ed. part of our training. Foot-racing and all that.'

'And he swallowed it?'

'If you mean did he drop the subject, yes.' Paddy's

voice was cold. She felt cold.

Kip must have sensed her bleakness, for at once he set himself out to be considerate and charming.

'I'm a pig. I get so worked up over things. Forgive me, please forgive, my sweet. It's just that I love you so much ... Yes, I do, Padua ... I love you so much I see red if anything gets in my way, my way of escape.' He added: 'Escape with you.'

'I've told you, Kip, I love this place.'

'Yes, and with some money you could have your cake and eat it. We both could. Standen's up for sale.'

'Oh,' said Paddy, slowly seeing light, 'and you wanted me to time Into the Light so that you could decide how much to outlay on him?'

There was a pause, then Kip said: 'Why yes, darling, all I was thinking of was a wager. I haven't much, but if his time was good, I'd put the whole lot on, and at least we'd have a deposit.' He ruffled Paddy's acorn hair.

'It's not strictly right,' said Paddy judiciously, 'but I suppose on the other hand watching a horse to see how much you *dare* isn't such a sin.'

'Darling, you've put it perfectly. Padua—forgive?'

She forgave him. She had tea with him in the Standen house. She kissed him back when he kissed her goodbye. When, as a final gesture, he took the watch from her and said: 'Darling, I'm giving this to one of the hands. Your distress just now really shocked me. Nothing, just nothing is worth your unhappiness,' Paddy knew she loved Kip. He had capitulated so completely, even though he had wanted desperately to win a few dollars. What a man, she thought, completely forgetting that changed, unpleasant face. Right from the beginning he has helped me. When everyone was down with the virus and I left the stud keys in the box he even took time off from his own work to save the situation.

Yes, Kip was fine, and Kip loved her, and she——

I love Kip, Paddy said.

During that week she set herself out to get to know her boys. Her knowledge was only sketchy of the wards so far. She had been a little distressed in the beginning when she had learned that two of them had already left school and that the other two frankly were anticipating their release. She even had written down to Mr Aston about it.

The principal had written back recommending Chapter Seven of their manual to Paddy, and Paddy had studied it assiduously. The aim now, she absorbed, was not to oblige a child to stop at school if he honestly and wholeheartedly did not want that. Many children did not want it, so left and made an equal success of their lives as their more scholarly contemporaries—often a greater success. They seemed to value education more when it was not thrust upon them. Paddy could have backed that up now with her own experience, for Richard and Paul were *very* dedicated evening scholars. They had told her that to get on in a stable you needed something on top as well as elsewhere.

'I presume by that you mean your head?' Paddy had said once.

'Yes, and by the other we mean our——'

'Yes, I follow. That will be enough.'

Paddy made it her business to attend the valley school, and inquire about her juniors, and the report was good. Steady boys but not scholastically minded. Never tertiary stuff. The signs were always obvious even quite early in a child's learning years. The teacher repeated the manual's view that certain minors do better *after* they have left their place of learning.

'They're very ambitious,' Paddy was assured.

'Ambitious about horses?'

'That needs know-how, too, and they'll realise and work on that, I think.'

Something on top as well as elsewhere, Paddy had grinned to herself, but she had accepted the fact that it takes both sides to make up a world.

She began going across to the stables with her four, enjoying their enthusiasm and beginning to become very enthusiastic herself. She was amazed at the way Melisande's foal had grown since Magnus had introduced the little, soft-eyed girl, why, she was now quite a young lady.

'The sire Quick as Lightning is a whopper of a horse,' explained Paul, 'so that accounts for her long legs.'

'They are very long.' Paddy was enchanted with the lovely, still gauche, restless child beside the sedate Melisande. 'She must be very young still and yet she has reached that height.'

'She's one,' said John.

'Oh, no!'

'Yes, she is, all horses have their birthdays on the first of August and since the foal was dropped' ... Paddy smiled secretly at the knowledgeable word ... 'just before August she's already one. Even eligible for the Sires Produce this year, and that could lead to anywhere, even the Plateau Plate.'

'Yes, and Magnus is letting Paul have a first go with her to get her used to the idea. He thinks she'll even challenge her half-brother Into the Light one day. We do, too. We expect a lot from Melisande's Girl—that's her name. Oh, yes, she'll put Into the Light into the shade. I say that's good, isn't it? Into the Light into the shade.' Richard had to repeat it to the others.

He showed Paddy how Melisande's foal had taken to the saddle, but before he could do it someone had to stand beside the blind mare and talk to and soothe her. The most placid of mothers, it only took the absence of her baby to agitate her into a near-hysteria. Paddy had never seen an equal panic in any animal.

'What will you do when Melisande's Girl really races?' Paddy asked the boys. 'You can't always have someone around reassuring her. She's intelligent, you can see that, she will soon catch on that she's standing alone.'

'She'll have another baby by then, Magnus has mated her with Dashing Duke.'

'Well now,' smiled Paddy, patting Melisande's head and looking into Melisande's unseeing, cream-covered blind eyes, 'you're a chosen girl—nobility no less!'

Paddy enjoyed watching the boys exercising the filly; then once when Bill, the head man, permitted Paul to do a spell with Into the Light she was as excited as he was. She even wished she had that wretched stopwatch with her, but, glancing up the straight to watch how Paul was doing, she briefly glimpsed a flash of light and knew that someone *had* brought a stopwatch. Also binoculars. She caught the twin glimpse of the lenses. At once there was nothing there, but in that brief moment Paddy, too, had recognised Kip Norris. Well, as she had remarked before, it was not good perhaps, but it was not really a sin.

It was a pleasant week, but somehow a waiting week. Waiting for Magnus David? Then at the end of the seven days Magnus came back.

The boys greeted him eagerly, they had lots to tell him about every four-footed member of the stable—especially at this juncture the white-haired boy, the Yoothamurra hope, Into the Light.

'Yes,' said Magnus, 'and I've been seeing how the white hopes of the big-time stables are guarded in Sydney. Security is very high there. I don't like to do the same here, after all, we've never needed to, but if we did——' He paused. 'Have any of you ever seen anyone around?'

'No,' they chorused.

Magnus turned to Paddy. 'You, Miss Travis?'

'No.'

. . . So another lie was added to the list.

When the boys and Paddy turned to leave, Magnus kept Paddy back. He was helping himself to a brandy and soda, and his eyes looked narrowly across at her over the balloon glass. He did not offer her anything, not even a sherry, he knew she would refuse, but she felt she should have been asked nonetheless.

'Have you told the kids about the National Trust?' he questioned.

'I have mentioned it, but when I mentioned, too, the possibility of their living in the stud quarters they were very excited, and, I'm afraid, not unduly distressed over the Trust.'

'That's all right. In fact it's as it should be. They're young and anxious for new things, not old. But you, too, will be going. Are you anxious for the new?'

Instinctively Paddy replied with affection: 'But the banana house isn't new, is it?' She realised what she had said, and added hastily: 'Though I know, of course, I won't be there.'

He still stood with the balloon glass in his hand. He

had lifted it up before she spoke, but at her words he had kept it poised there. She could see his face through the crystal, she could see his eyes.

'Of course,' he said evenly. 'Now for your briefing.'

'Briefing?' she queried.

'We're having house guests. Five members of the Trust will be arriving here quite soon to stay several days while they look over the place, check what will need to be done.'

'I see. And as house-mother you would like me to keep to my own quarters, keep the wards in theirs?'

'Don't be ridiculous, looking over Yoothamurra means looking over its entirety, not just several rooms. In the finished reconstruction the house will be as it was in the beginning, no divisions for three different household functions. The Trust will naturally need to see every room, so how can you isolate yourself?'

'Then you don't want me there? Perhaps I could take the boys down to the plantation.'

'Having the boys down at the plantation isn't such a bad idea, but the other suggestion is out of the question, for when they arrive I will naturally need you to establish them, be the hostess.'

Paddy protested, 'But I'm a house-mother, not a hostess.'

'You can pour tea, can't you? Make polite remarks concerning the weather? I've arranged about the cooking, and a couple of valley girls have agreed to come in and help.'

'I still think as a house-mother——' But Paddy got no further. He had put down the brandy glass and taken several steps towards her.

'As your employer, which I am, Miss Travis, for

though Closer Families may have trained you they don't call the tune any more, you'll do what I ask.'

'I think you mean call, like in call the tune, because you're calling it loud and clear.'

'So long as you hear it like that.'

'Oh, I do!'

'Then do what it bids.'

This time Paddy did not answer. Sulkily she turned away, only to be turned promptly and forcibly back.

'These are nice people coming,' said Magnus David, 'and I want them treated nicely. Understand?'

'Can a house-mother understand niceties?' she retorted.

'A house-mother will, or——'

'Or?'

'Just try to be nice,' he said. 'They won't be young, but they'll be very genuine, very earnest, very sensitive people.'

'Yes, sir.'

'And take that look off your face!'

'Yes, sir.'

What she would have done then Paddy, rather astounded herself at her impertinence, could not have said. She even recoiled a step in trepidation.

Then there was the sound of several cars pulling up on the drive outside, and Magnus, who had angrily advanced even further on her, turned round and strode to the door, then went out.

Paddy did not follow him, not then. She decided she would wait until she was asked. But she did go to the window to look out.

Six, not five, people were getting out of two cars, and the sixth did *not* look as Magnus had described.

Instead, she was young. Also, she was beautiful.

'Very genuine, very earnest, very sensitive' ... wasn't that what you said, Mr David?

Oh, no, kind sir, not *that* one.

CHAPTER TWELVE

BY the time Paddy reached the patio, Magnus was at the bottom of the steps greeting his visitors. He did not glance promptly up at her as Paddy had rather expected, instead his attention was on the youngest member of the group. On the exceptionally beautiful ... and Paddy observed that now ... girl.

To her surprise, for it seemed rather an unusual way to meet a member of a Trust, Magnus kissed her. Had Paddy been a moment before she would have seen it was in reply to the girl's kiss, but all Paddy saw was a handshake all round to the rest of the Trust from Magnus, then for the girl—a kiss.

They all climbed the stairs. There were general introductions, then the allocation of bedrooms, after which Magnus asked genially if they would all assemble in the big lounge for talk and drinks.

'You see,' he said to Paddy when they had gone, 'I'm not even giving you any tea-pouring, so there's no need to wear that look.'

'What look?'

'A disagreeably surprised look.'

'I don't know about disagreeable, but I am surprised. The youngest member is not at all as you described.'

147

'No, she's not,' he agreed calmly.

'Then how——'

'I've known Anthea for years ... yes, she's Anthea Cope ... and I ran into her in Sydney.'

'And asked her along as well.'

'No, she actually does belong to the Trust.' A pause and a slight smile. 'To the social side, not the restoration. All such functions require a social side.'

'So you made this pilgrimage social as well as informative?'

'Look' ... an irritated frown ... 'she has every right to be here and you have no right to comment. Probably you've been the only rose on the bush so long you can't bear another bud.'

'Why, thank you, Mr David, no one has ever called me a rose before.'—But someone had called her a flower, a a lot of flowers. Kip had said : 'All the flowers of spring.' But Kip's offering had been sincere, and this from Magnus was deliberate sarcasm.

There were steps and the visitors began filing into the room again. Magnus got busy at the bar, Paddy carrying the tray for him. Mostly they took an inch of sherry, but the bud ... he had said that ... asked for something on the rocks.

Paddy, suddenly restless and reckless, asked for a balloon glass of brandy for herself.

'Your balloon has gone up,' Magnus answered quietly, 'take a small sherry and shut up about it.'

'And if I don't?'

'Here you are, Miss Travis.' He put the glass in Paddy's hand. 'Mrs Linfoot, would you like our Padua Travis, house-mother to my four wards here but now acting hostess for me, to give you a quick look around?'

All the Trust except Anthea said they would like that very much, and they followed Paddy.

They were, as Magnus had told her, genuine, earnest, sincere, nice people. (Paddy did not know yet about the one who had not tagged on.) She enjoyed conducting them.

It was the same in the several days that followed, days when the Trust, when not sketching and measuring and mentally renovating and restoring, happily followed her on walks round the garden, through the bush, over to the stables and stud. On the last occasion Anthea came, too.

There were oohs and ahs of delight as they were permitted to stroke the noble brows of the Yoothamurra thoroughbreds. There were blurred eyes as Melisande summoned her daughter to her side then the mare and the filly cantered round the paddock. Into the light brought more admiration. Even the stable dogs, and a kitten who had attached herself to Golden Wedding's box and to Golden Wedding, inspired applause.

All the time Paddy could not help noticing that Anthea kept looking around as though in search of something— or somebody. At last the girl came and asked carelessly:

'Last time I was here there was a different trainer.'

'I wouldn't know,' said Padua. 'I've only been here myself a short while.'

'Name of Norris.' The girl was looking at her now with narrowed eyes, and Paddy realised it would be no good to try an evasion, not with someone like this.

'Yes, I know a Mr Norris. Kip Norris.'

'Where is he?'

'He left Yoothamurra before I came. He's at Standen, the neighbouring stud.'

149

'I would know Standen, of course,' said Anthea. 'I know all the places here. My grandparents had an estate on the plateau and I used to come up at school breaks.' A tiptilted, rather secret smile. 'So that trainer left? Why?'

'I would hardly know that, would I?'

'No, you wouldn't, not a house employee as you are, but I did think you might have heard.'

Paddy did not reply and a few moments went by.

'Of course I haven't been up for a long while,' continued Anthea, 'I've been overseas. When I came back I decided to pick up the threads again ... social threads, I mean. I lived very much before my overseas stay in the social whirl. But all my friends had moved on, I found, and—well, it wasn't so simple. That's why I joined the more frivolous side of the Trust. I had to have a toehold. But they're a dreary crowd, aren't they? I expect you've been wondering how I fitted in.'

'Not really,' Paddy lied. 'As I'm out of my depth in my present capacity of hostess, my time has been fully taken up trying to do a job I don't know anything about.'

'That,' nodded Anthea, 'was apparent from the first. You're Children, aren't you?'

'Yes, you could say that.'

'Even more dreary, surely, than the Trust old dears.'

Paddy shrugged, 'It's a matter of opinion.'

'Well, to my opinion it is, and Magnus must be off his head. Poor pet, though, it would be the trauma of Jeremy's passing. When he sees clearly again he'll change his mind.'

'I don't believe so. He's intending to adopt these boys.'

'I think you can forget that, Miss ... what was the name again?'

'Travis.'

'You can forget that now that I'm here,' said Anthea. 'In these last few days I've been reconsidering things, wondering if I do want the old bright régime after all, or if I want to settle down at Yoothamurra instead.' A pause. 'I've only to say one word, you know.' Anthea gave a soft, small laugh.

The ladies were gathering round Paddy again, she had no opportunity to answer Anthea—anyway, even if she had, what could she have said?

She wondered what was the next attraction she could offer, wondered quite miserably, which surprised her, for she had loved every minute of being a show-woman, loved it as much as they had loved being shown, but now she felt distinctly flat.

Magnus came to the rescue soon after with a proposal that even got Paddy out of her doldrums. Though the horse pool was invaluable, he told the ladies, it offered none of the invigoration of a gallop along a beach and then a dip in the surf. The ladies could be driven there to watch, and the horses could be ridden there to participate, and as the road wound round the mountains but the track went over the mountains ... a brief reminding glance at Paddy ... they could both arrive at the same time. Would the Trust like that?

Oh, yes, they all liked that.

They left early the next morning, the ladies and Paddy in the two cars following the posse of riders. Posse was not the right word, Paddy knew, but she had not expected so many horses, so many horsemen.—One of them a horse*woman*. Anthea was not being driven, she was riding, riding Rest Assured, the handsome brown colt that Magnus had told Paddy he reserved for special visitors *who could ride*.

Anthea could certainly ride, and she certainly knew it. She handled Rest Assured, who loved to be the focus, with all the assurance of someone who loves to be the focus as well. Paddy heard soft mutterings behind her, for Anthea was not popular, but she was more absorbed in her own thoughts. What an utter greenhorn Magnus must have thought her after a rider like this!

They started off, but for some reason Anthea dawdled. Perhaps Magnus was in the rear, Paddy deduced.

She herself kept up a stream of informative chatter for the ladies. This stud they were now approaching was Standen, as big and as thriving a concern as Yootha-murra. She saw that Anthea was not just dawdling now, but had all but stopped. She also noted that Magnus was a long way to the *front*.

Then Kip stepped out from a stable, and Paddy half-raised her hand to answer his salute. Then she saw he was not looking in her direction, he was looking in Anthea's. She saw Anthea raise her crop and keep it there a moment, then the girl dug in her heels and caught up with the rest of the riders, and within minutes the horses were going Indian file over the edge then down the mountain track.

Magnus was right. The two parties arrived at the coast together, and then followed one of the most delightful scenes that Paddy had ever watched. Up and down the deserted beach the horses galloped, then, when the sweat was shining on their lovely coats, they received their reward—a plunge in the dancing blue surf. That they loved it was very apparent, several even let out whickers of pleasure. They cropped afterwards on the grasses that grew right down to the sand and while they did so Paddy helped Magnus boil some billies and barbecue big steaks.

Paddy was quiet now. It was not that her pleasure had left her but that she was feeling something she could not have explained. Something about this place. A familiarity somehow. Familiarity?

'Where are we?' she asked Magnus at last.

'On the beach.'

'What beach?'

'Do you want the latitude and longitude?'

'No, just where. That is if you know where.'

'I should. It's ours ... I mean mine ... now. It's the adjoining bay to Pelican.'

'Pelican?' she queried.

'Didn't you recognise the headland?'

'No.'

'You were too busy on other things, then?'

'I've been helping you, haven't I?' she said.

'I meant—then.'

In as hard a voice as his, Paddy answered: 'Yes. Too busy. Does that satisfy you, Mr David?'

The horses and riders left soon after. This time, because of the steep ascent, they would take much longer than the cars. Magnus went first, then right at the end, as before, Anthea cantered by on Rest Assured. The cars gave them an hour, then left as well.

The horses made good time. When the motor transport reached the plateau they were a distant blob turning into the Yoothamurra gates. But as they sped past Standen, Paddy saw one mount which had not reached Yoothamurra yet. Rest Assured was cropping between two of the Standen stables. And had the colt not reached

153

for something succulent he must have seen, Paddy would not have noticed him, for the outbuildings were rather concealed from the road.

For a few moments she was shaken out of her abstraction. Ever since Magnus had said: 'Pelican, didn't you recognise it?' and had followed it with: 'You were too busy on other things then?' she had been very miserable.

Remember September, she had been thinking, remember fun and uninvolvement and simplicity, no subtleties, no doubts, no innuendoes as now.

But suddenly she was wondering about the rider of Rest Assured, about Anthea, who recalled 'a different trainer', for that was all she had said. 'A different trainer.'

But for all her apparent uninterest Anthea had stopped earlier today to salute Kip, and this afternoon she had paused again, then even gone into Standen.

'It's been an enjoyable outing,' the Trust dears were saying appreciatively. 'We'll hate leaving tomorrow.'

'*She* isn't leaving,' one of the members said tartly.

'Well, being on the social side, I expect——'

Paddy barely heard their discussion. The fact that Anthea was stopping on was fully occupying her.

It could only mean one thing, she knew. What had Anthea told her?—'I have only to say one word, you know.' Obviously Anthea had meant——

Well, Paddy could believe that. Magnus David was certainly very considerate to Anthea, and they had been close friends all their lives.

But where did Kip come in? And why? If Anthea only recalled him as 'a different trainer' why was she going out of her way to see him, as it appeared she was?

'Yes, very sorry, dear.' Paddy realised that the ladies

were still talking about leaving tomorrow.

'I'm sorry, too,' she stirred herself to say, and she *was*. Sorry, if what she was thinking was true, *for Magnus*. She did not like Magnus, she would never like Magnus, but she didn't want things to be like that for him.

'Sorry, too,' Paddy said again.

The ladies left the next morning, telling Magnus what a wonderful time he had given them, and what a wonderful subject Yoothamurra would make for preservation for posterity. Paddy stood beside Magnus to see that all the bags were stacked in, the ladies tucked in, and to wave. Anthea did not come down. Paddy noticed this at once, she had wondered several times if the Trust members, restorative side, had only been supposing among themselves when they had said that Miss Cope would not be leaving. But no, the girl was not among them.

As the two cars went off, Paddy said with assumed innocence: 'There seems more room than when they came up. My goodness, one of them is missing—the pretty one. Stop the cars. She must have slept in.'

'Drop it,' Magnus advised shortly. 'You know as well as I do that Anthea is staying on.'

'She is?'

'In one minute I'll do to you what should have been done regularly as a child but obviously wasn't.' He was quite furious, and Paddy decided to do what he said, to 'drop it', though why it should make him *that* angry she did not know.

She turned and went up the steps into the house, but Magnus did not follow, he strode off in the direction of the stables.

When she went into Yoothamurra, Paddy found

Anthea waiting for her. She must have been waiting, for she sat intentionally on a chair opposite the door.

'Just a moment, Miss Travis,' she halted.

'It will have to be that, Miss Cope,' said Paddy. 'I'm anxious to get back to my own work, not the work that's been thrust on me these last few days.'

Anthea's face dropped perceptibly, which made Paddy think it was on that subject she had wished to speak to the house-mother turned hostess.

A little sulkily Anthea admitted: 'You've beaten me to it. I just wanted to say you can keep to your own side now, to your own job. I'll take over here.'

'Gladly. I'm late with my report to Mr Aston, and Closer Families takes a dim view of that. I'll have our principal coming up here after me.'

'Which would be a change, anyway, from a parcel of women. Oh, the boredom! But it's over now, and Magnus and I can get down to some productive thinking.'

'I thought the house discussions were very productive,' said Paddy.

'I mean talk not punctuated with renovations and restorations and whatever. Private talk. It will be good to be civilised again. No more scratch meals collected at a servery window.'

'Well, there were only two girls available, and you could hardly expect them——'

'Dinner by candlelight,' Anthea smiled dreamily. She asked less dreamily: 'What kind of cook is your Mrs Dermott? Oh, yes, I know you don't do the meals yourself—quite the pampered house-mother, aren't you? But can she do other things as well as fill up greedy adolescents?'

'I'd class her as a good boy cook,' said Paddy judiciously. 'She's certainly excellent on stews and dumplings and——'

'Perish the thought!' Anthea shuddered. 'But perhaps it's just that she hadn't had an appreciative audience, I mean people who like finer things.'

'No, perhaps not,' said Paddy, a little surprised, for she could not imagine Mrs Dermott wanting to extend herself any more than she extended herself now. She had said often she was only doing her service for the wards.

'Have you asked Mrs Dermott yet?' Paddy inquired.

'No, but she'll come, of course. I'm afraid it will mean that you'll have to cook for your four and yourself when it happens, but after all you came here with that expectancy no doubt.'

'Yes,' said Paddy, 'but I still think you should feel out Mrs Dermott. She's not left the kitchen yet, but she should be about ready to go.'

'When she looks after just Magnus and me she won't go at all,' Anthea smiled. 'Go and tell her I'd like to see her.'

'I don't think——' What Paddy *was* thinking was that Anthea was putting a wrong foot forward right from the start. Mrs Dermott was a very independent person, she would not like being bidden.

Mrs Dermott didn't, but she came ... and refused the job. It was all over in a few minutes, Mrs Dermott out of the house, and Anthea near tears at her setback.

'I'll speak to Magnus about her. Such impudence! Is there someone else around? You should know, you live here.'

'I haven't for long,' Paddy reminded her.

'And won't for long either,' Anthea said crossly. She

thought a moment. 'Is the prepared food she brings to you and the wards any good?'

'We like it very much.'

'Could it pass, suitably embellished, then washed down with a good wine, for us?'

'Mutton Hotpot with vintage '39?' considered Paddy. 'Yes, I think it would.'

'You're being deliberately impertinent!' snapped Anthea.

Paddy said, 'Actually I'm trying to help. You have an idea there. I could tell Mrs Dermott to bring more, she'd love that, she adores filling up boys, then you could snitch some and do the embellishing.'

'Yes,' agreed Anthea, 'I'm sure I could do that.'

'And of course,' Paddy continued, 'there's always the club.'

But Anthea was fired with Paddy's first suggestion now. 'It's presentation,' she said, 'that counts, and I certainly have plenty of that.'

'You have,' agreed Paddy. 'Then I'll run after Mrs D. and tell her how ravenous the boys have become, shall I?'

She hurried out.

There were extra containers of food the next morning, and when Paddy passed them over, though Anthea grimaced she still supposed that with a curl of parsley, a shred of mint, a ring of capsicum, this, that, what-have-you, they would not be too awful.

This went on several days, then either Anthea's imagination went flat or she could not face the simpler offerings any more, for she sought out Paddy and told her to go back to the original rations.

'We're going to dine out,' she announced.

'Very nice,' nodded Paddy.

Anthea narrowed her beautiful eyes on Paddy. 'You sound knowledgeable.'

'I am.'

'And whom did you dine with?'

'Mr David took me.'

'Of course, naturally he would feel obliged to do that for a new employee.'

'There were many of the racing fraternity there, including' ... Paddy said it with careful carelessness, though she could not have said why she was going to such pains ... 'Mr Norris.'

'Kip goes?'

'He was there,' Paddy said again.

'Awkward,' commented Anthea, 'but then he has a fund of commonsense.'

'Mr David or Mr Norris?'

'Miss Travis, it has nothing to do with you.'

'No, it hasn't. I'll tell Mrs D. then, tell her some lie that the boys are putting on too much weight.'

'Tell them what you like,' yawned Anthea, and she turned and left.

Around seven Paddy heard the car moving away from Yoothamurra. She went to the window and saw it leave the drive and take the road to the club.

She was preoccupied all that evening, resulting in Mark asking her had a cat got her tongue and starting a general argument as to whether a cat, fast though it was, could get a tongue.

She pictured the corner table under the palm and Anthea looking out and possibly seeing Kip as she had seen him. Would Kip make up something to get rid of Magnus and allow him to dance with Anthea? Then when Magnus returned would he dance with Anthea himself? Would he—would he kiss her?

'If you're not going to eat that piece of pie, can I have it?' Paul cajoled.

'No, me, you're going to be a jockey, you have to stop at one slice.' It was Richard.

'No, me!' Mark.

'Me, Paddy!' John.—They all had dropped 'Miss' within a week.

Paddy passed over her untouched sweets, not bothering who got it. Kip dancing with Anthea, she was thinking. Magnus dancing with Anthea.

She found herself flinching over one of her thoughts, shrugging over the other, not being able to face up to what comprised the flinch and which the shrug.

Because the boys were beginning to look curiously at her, she made an effort, and smiled over both.

CHAPTER THIRTEEN

THREE days went by with Paddy seeing neither Anthea nor Magnus on their side of Yoothamurra, and three nights with only quick glimpses of them as they went off to the country club for dinner.

However, Magnus was attending the stables as usual, the boys reported, and was, they bitterly agreed, as sharp as a clump of scotch thistle with them.

'Picks on you for the smallest thing,' complained Paul.

'Like forgetting to clean, or sweep, or feed, or water,' reproved Paddy.

'The *smallest* thing,' repeated Paul. 'Isn't that right, Richard?'

'Since the bird's been here he's been a fair cow,' Richard concurred.

'Lamentable English, Richard, and both of you watch your tongues!' ordered Paddy sternly.

They grimaced but obeyed.

They were good boys, and Paddy could not help feeling angry at the treatment they reported from Magnus David. If the man was annoyed, he should take his annoyance out on someone else. She had a mind to write a contra report to Closer Families, but after all a snarl or two did not comprise maltreatment, and when a patron gave so very generously ... Perhaps if she spoke to the boss——

She had an opportunity that afternoon, the first for many days. Magnus David came striding up the front path, pushing the wide-brimmed hat he always wore to the back of his head, and Paddy quickly made it her business at that moment to be leaving the house.

They almost collided.

'Mr David, I——'

'Miss Travis, the very person I wanted to see.'

They said it together.

'You first,' he indicated.

But now that she was face to face with him, Paddy could not word her complaint as she wished. She could hardly say: 'Paul reports to me that your temper is awful and Richard says it's because of your bird,' and for the life of her she could think of nothing else.

Impatiently he came in: 'While you're working it out I must tell you that I've decided that you and the boys are to have a week down at the banana house.

There's a school break coming up, and the senior pair are still young enough to enjoy a holiday. So tomorrow, Miss Travis, you can push off.'

'Oh—oh, thank you,' Paddy said weakly.

'Have you found your words yet?'

'I don't think I need them now, I was just going to ask you if the boys were getting on your nerves, because they've told me that you—well——'

'That I'm irritating them?'

'Yes,' Paddy said.

'The answer is no. I'm just struggling through a sticky patch at present. When I get out of it again I'll be the same.'

'Can—can I help?' she asked.

He looked down at her, visibly surprised at her offer, and Paddy felt ashamed. How unfriendly and how unsympathetic do I appear to him? she thought.

'That's kind of you, and yes, you could, only of course you can't.' A pause. 'And wouldn't.'

'What answer is that?'

'What you make of it,' he said. 'You can tell the kids the news, then begin packing up your supplies. You can take the bigger car so as to fit everything in. You can leave first thing.'

'Thank you, Mr David.'

The boys were mildly excited about it all. They preferred the plateau, but the valley came as a pleasant change, especially with the surf within reach.

'Besides,' said Paul, 'when we get back he might be a decent bloke again.'

'And the bird gone,' added Richard.

They took more food than clothes, for they would stay in jeans and skivvies all the time, but food could

162

not be bought, so had to be brought. Magnus put in frozen meat, frozen bread, and said that the vegetable patch at the banana house would supplement these items, and the ever-present bananas, of course, finish it all off.

'I could do,' he said seriously, 'with some Banana Flambé myself.'

'Perhaps Miss Cope——' began Paddy.

'Perhaps you would like to keep your conjectures to yourself.'

It did not take long to descend the valley, though it did take a lot of concentration. John pronounced triumphantly that they rounded four entire mountains before they finally reached the plantation.

But once there it was worth every applied minute. The days here came sparklingly fresh, laced with the tang of the sea not very far away, the lovely banana coast, warm with hillsides drowsing in the sun, cool from mountains with battalions of trees rising sheer from the valley bottom.

Then the banana palms! Up they climbed and down they dipped, shining green trees with great hands of fruit ripening under silver, clear and blue bags, the heat and humidity of these bags forming a personal 'hot house' for each giant bunch. The silver, Paddy learned, was to prevent the very hot summer burning of fruit, the clear to enable the grower to judge the maturity for harvesting purposes without opening the bag, and the cornflower blue was all purpose and all seasons.

The man who came in to keep an eye on the plantation told Paddy ruefully that banana growers had to have weak heads and strong backs, both very necessary when you made bananas your job. But he said it with a laugh, and Paddy knew he would not have changed for the world. He let the boys operate the flying fox, a means of delivering bunches to the packing sheds by wires. These strong wires were fastened to posts outside the packing shed, and, at the opposite end, to another post or tree stump. The boys had rides up and down, but Richard, descending, got stuck some metres above the ground level, and, waiting to be rescued, spent his time pelting the others with the ripest fruit he could find. When Paddy discovered that banana stain was impossible to remove, she stopped all that.

But it was a wonderful break. All she had felt when Magnus had first brought her here flooded back again. The house was full of friendly ghosts; she almost found herself talking to them.

She had brought Magnus's mother's banana cookbook, and soon the boys were as keen on banana meat pie and banana casserole as they were on Mrs Dermott's more orthodox things. She was making banana curry the morning Magnus came down.

Paddy's first thought was Anthea, who presumably would be with him; she simply could not see Anthea liking banana curry.

But Magnus was alone, and Magnus evidently did. He stood at the door and he sighed ecstatically: 'Shades of Steak Diane and Burgundy Veal—give me any hour, any day, any year, banana curry. Paprika, coriander, chilli, and, of course, bananas. Oh, that smell! I could almost love you for it, girl.'

'Thank you,' said Paddy. She added cautiously: 'I suppose I do say thanks?'

'It all depends, doesn't it?' But he said it carelessly, and they didn't follow it up. 'How have the boys been?' he went on.

'Drinking up every moment. I think you might have lost a book-keeper and a jockey, not to mention several strappers.'

'But gained some banana growers?'

'Weak heads and strong backs,' she laughed.

'Oh, so you heard that.'

'Have you come to take us home?' she asked.

'Yes, but not till tomorrow. I'll stay the night here myself.'

'Anthea——' She must have gone, Paddy was thinking thankfully.

'She's all right. I've managed to get a housekeeper. Those club dinners were getting me down. Don't I look thinner?'

'It could be the dancing,' Paddy suggested.

'It couldn't be, I didn't dance. But I think' ... a cocked ear and a smile ... 'I could be persuaded to now. Where in Betsy did the boys find the old phonograph?'

The music, shrill and tinny yet oddly sweet, came hopping in from the next room. It was *The Blue Danube*, and apart from a hiccough now and then it still rang true.

'According to my programme, you promised me this waltz,' Magnus bowed.

'Strange,' frowned Paddy, 'I distinctly remember giving it to Sir Basil.'

'The pox to Sir Basil, you promised me.' He took her in his arms and began moving round the room to the delighted applause of the boys who had come to the door to watch.

They played games after dinner, games people did not play now, Consequences with outrageous happenings to friends and acquaintances being disclosed at the unfolding of closely scribbled sheets, after that finding things and spinning things and doing things that belonged to this old house and belonged to then, not to new houses and now.

'It's been wonderful,' Paddy said when it was all over.

'For me as well,' Magnus nodded.

'A pity——'

'Yes?'

But Paddy would not finish it. She blurted: 'I forget what I was going to say.'

'I don't think you do, but if you want it like that, then forget. Well, forget, anyway, until you remember.'

Remember September! It was not said, but it was as distinct in the old room as though it had been spoken, spoken loud and clear.

They stood silent a moment, then Magnus turned, called 'Goodnight, all,' and went to his room. At the other end of the house, the boys between them, Paddy went to hers.

They went back to Yoothamurra the next day, and it all began again. The silence in the master unit, the very occasional glimpses of the occupants, especially now that there was someone cooking for Anthea and Magnus and Paddy no longer glimpsed them leaving at night for the club.

The Plateau Plate was approaching, and an air of excitement was taking over the sleepy top of the hill ... top of four hills, Paddy corrected herself.

Horses never seen here before were being exercised, for interstate entrants were arriving continuously to be stabled wherever a niche could be found for them, and then acclimatised. Yoothamurra itself had provided boxes for three. Clusters of cars could be seen every day. Most of the participants stayed on the coast and travelled up, but a few camped, and some of the smaller studs, glad of a sideline, accommodated the rest.

Cup fever took over, and Richard ... after all, he was nearly a man ... got it badly.

'The fellers tell me it's wonderful at the club of a night,' he told Paddy once.

'Yes, it would be extra bright now.'

'I'd love to go.'

'Well, Richard, I don't think Mr David would object.'

'He wouldn't—he said so. It isn't that.'

'Money?' asked Paddy.

'I've saved up.'

'Then?'

'A bird—I'm sorry, Paddy, a girl.'

'That's better,' she smiled.

A pause. A long one.

'*You* are a girl,' Richard pointed out.

'True.'

'Would you come with me?'

'Oh, Richard dear, I'm too old for you.'

'Oh, I know that,' said Richard cruelly, though no doubt unconscious of any cruelty, 'but the fellers say a man looks a fool without a bird—I mean without a girl.'

'I'm sure you could get lots of girls,' Paddy told him.

'Maybe, but where?'

'There'll be plenty at the club.'

'Yes, but I have to get there first, haven't I, without looking that fool the fellers said.'

'Richard, I do believe you are proposing to take me, then dump me!' she smiled.

'Well, Paddy, you're good-looking enough to get plenty of men yourself.'

'You really think so?' Paddy laughed, but she listened with woman-keenness for his reply.

'You're all right,' he said.

'Then, Sir Galahad, my answer to you is Yes.'

'You'll come?'

'I said so.'

'No kidding?'

'You watch for me tonight!'

Because he was young and because such things matter to these young, Paddy put on *everything*. When she saw Richard's face, she knew the effort had been worthwhile.

'I reckon,' said Richard, 'those young girls can look elsewhere.'

'A pity for you, then, because *I'll* be looking elsewhere.'

Richard grinned and led the way to the old roadster he had borrowed from another hand.

The club was certainly much more alive than it had been when Magnus had brought her. Richard, after a horrified glance at the menu, thankfully accepted Paddy's plea that she was not hungry and that a sandwich would be fine, and very soon, in spite of his declaration about young girls, found himself in the middle of them.

Paddy sat back and prepared to enjoy herself watching the floor. She did not watch long. Kip came up to her.

'Padua, where have you been hiding yourself?. I haven't seen you for days.'

'We went down to the valley, Kip, but apart from that it's been awkward. We had the Trust up, and then Anthea Cope decided to stay on. She's still here.'

'Is she now?' he said without any show of interest, and lit a cigarette. 'I've missed you,' he told her. 'Shall we dance?'

'No, I don't think so. You see, Magnus David saw through your ruse last time.'

'Is he here now? Surely not. Surely he's not parted from Miss Cope?'

'No,' said Paddy, aware, and angry, at a hurt as she admitted it, 'Richard brought me. As he's still only a child I hardly think——'

'Of course, dear, I understand perfectly.' Kip was being very nice, but then he was nice. 'That's Richard there, isn't it?'

'Yes.'

'He's having the time of his life. That little peach is a strapper at Lewin's Stud. Lewin employs girls. Pretty kid, isn't she?'

'Very.' Paddy tried but did not succeed in concealing a sigh.

'Not jealous, surely?' Kip asked.

'No, tired, and by the look of Richard——'

'You're not going to budge him, you're thinking? Well, why budge him? Why not beckon him over and tell him you have another way to get home so he's on his own? I'm sure he'd appreciate that.'

'Yes, I believe he would. But Kip, don't stand around while I do it, you know how Standen is considered by Yoothamurra.'

'I know,' Kip laughed, and strolled away.

When Paddy told Richard he was at first very righteous and offering to leave, but quite soon, at Paddy's insistence, anxious to stay on.

'I really am tired, Richard. And here, take this.' Paddy pressed some dollar notes on him. After all, it was his first night out with any girl.

'Oh, Paddy!' Richard said.

Kip had his car door open, and they drove slowly back in the perfumed night.

'Exciting time, isn't it?' They were passing a paddock that had been turned over to camping, and already the tents were thick.

'Very,' agreed Paddy. 'And to think one of our visitors ... I'm meaning the four-legged variety now ... may take out the Plateau Plate, and neither your Peerless Prince nor our Into the Light be the victor after all.'

'Possible, but very unlikely. Our boyos have the advantage of being on their own home ground. Besides, their times are superb.'

'Yes, *you* would know that,' smiled Paddy in the darkness, 'I saw you one day with your stopwatch timing Into the Light.'

'Thank you, then, for not telling on me.' Kip had stopped the car to light a cigarette, but he leaned over first and kissed her. It was funny how it meant nothing, Paddy thought, and evidently, by its lightness, meant little to him as well.

'You've been a great kid,' Kip went on. 'Look at the web of deceit you spun for me.'

Paddy stirred uneasily. Kip's voice was bright, but there was something as well as brightness there. A kind of—warning? Keep doing what you've already done, it seemed to say, or——

'Kip——' she began.

'Darling?'

'I——' But Paddy could not find the words.

Kip could though. He said in that same voice again: 'Keep being that great kid, Padua. When I think of what you've done——'

'Have I?'

'Oh, yes, indeed you have.'

'But what, Kip?'

He would not tell her. He took her to the gate of Yoothamurra and let her out.

'If I don't manage to see you before the Plate, may the best nag win,' he grinned.

'Not nag, Kip.'

'No, sweetest, may the best of the bunch ... and Prince and Light ... win. I think I know which, don't you?' He winked.

She watched him go off, then went into the house, vaguely, inexplicably uneasy. She stood at the window waiting for his car to turn the bend to Standen, but though she stood for ten minutes that never happened.

He could not have turned it before she reached the window, she thought, it took longer than that, it took quite a while. She would not have been any time reaching her room and crossing to the window.

It was then she saw it, a very brief flash of light, then no light at all. It came from the stables. She stood waiting, but it never happened again, so she must have imagined it all.

She started to prepare for bed, but she felt terribly on edge, oddly nervous. Why hadn't she seen Kip's car turn the bend?

There was no guard at the stud, it was something that Magnus had stated for anyone to hear that he was reluctant to begin. They had never had anything happen like the things that happened in the city. Also, although the staff accommodation was close, the windows faced the opposite direction—intentionally so, Magnus had said; a man does not want to look on his hours off at what he looks at while he's at work.

Suddenly, not fully aware of what she was doing, Paddy was taking off the dress she had worn to impress Richard and putting on jeans instead, pulling over a shirt.

She found a torch, and went silently down the stairs and out of the house. Across to the stud. If for one minute she had thought about it, she would not have done anything so illogical, so incautious, so obviously ill-advised.

But Paddy did not think. She simply went.

Everything was obscure. At this time of the month the moon was a mere sliver, not even, as Mark, standing earlier by the window with her, had remarked, a shred of lemon. The stars, too, were covered with cloud, for up here it usually rained at some time in the dark hours producing later those unbelievably freshly-washed mornings. Paddy thought longingly of morning now, she was not at all keen on this black adventure. However, she knew the way and she was knowledgeable about each paddock, so it could have been worse. Quite frankly the worst thing just now was her strengthening idea that she was being an idiot. Since that initial flicker of light there had been nothing else. Paddy hesitated, then went to turn back. But at once she was walking forward again, for the light had flicked briefly a second time, and she suspected ... no, she felt certain ... it would be Kip. Somewhere along the lane in a thicket of trees she knew had she looked she would have found his car waiting while he—while he—— She moved more quickly now, she was not going to an assassin, a thief, she was going to Kip to ask him why. *Why*.

The light, she estimated, had come from the middle cluster of boxes ... from the shining hope's box. Well, though she still intended to be reproving about it, that made sense. Kip was very anxious to assess Into the Light, and since he was strictly forbidden to do so openly, he had now come secretly, it was as explainable and as basic as that. Kip was planning a kill, he had told her that, and if he was going to wager every cent he had it was only natural, if ill-advised, that he would be worried about the outcome. After all, he was not like Magnus David ... rich.

He would be concerned, yes, but should it be the extent of doing what he now had done, creeping in on the enemy camp to see for himself? Come to think of it ... a momentary halt ... how *had* he got this far? Over the paddocks perhaps, you only needed legs to climb fences for that, but *into the box*, as Paddy could see now by the small chink of light in the white hope's stable? How had Kip got *there*?

She moved forward, moved in, said something, she could not have told what, then heard something drop as Kip wheeled round.

He retrieved what he had held, at the same time gasping: 'Good lord, Padua, you scared the daylights out of me! What are you doing here?'

'That's what I came to ask you. Kip, are you mad?'

'I think I am.' Kip was being the young, caught-out schoolboy. 'The dogs could have got at me.'

'There are none,' Paddy reminded him. By that she meant there were only a few playful foxies, some sleepy old spaniels, no watchdogs. No guards; Magnus had preferred it like that.

'I still took a risk, but darling, I had to. I had to look your Son of Darkness over, compare him to our Prince.'

Paddy said crossly, 'He's called Into the Light.'

173

'Yes, my pet. Into the Light. You might remember the money I intend parting with, I just had to be sure.' A pause. A reminding pause. 'For us. And you, Padua, what brought you? And don't tell me a flick of light.' He had come close to her, and he bent over and kissed her meaningfully.

So it was just as she had thought, Paddy told herself, a reckless move but nothing at all in it. Then she remembered the open box door. Magnus always locked the stables—it was something he had impressed on the boys. Had he forgotten this time?

'But how did you get in, Kip?' she wanted to know.

If he had told her a lie, Paddy would probably have believed him. Everyone slips up at some time, and Kip had only to shrug that the door was ajar and the matter would have been closed.

But Kip, evidently weary of evasions, did not try lies any more.

'Are *you* asking me that?' he smirked back.

In the fitful light it was an unpleasant grin, and instinctively Paddy stepped back. At once he pulled her to where she had stood before, pulled her quite brutally.

'You gave me the key, remember?' he said.

'I did nothing of the sort. How could I? I never had a key.'

'While the virus was on you had, and you handed it to me to be duly impressed for any future need,' he said triumphantly.

'Kip, I didn't, you know I didn't!'

'You left it in a box with the instruction that when I'd finished with it I was to return it, so I returned it to the box. It doesn't take long' ... he shrugged ... 'to make an impression.'

'You copied the key for possible future use?'

'No, dear,' he corrected, '*we* copied it.'

'That's a lie!'

'Try convincing him,' Kip advised. 'Just try, Padua. Well, I've seen all I want of this chap now, and I know where my money is going. Come along, girl, don't stand there like a ghost.'

'You've made an accessory out of me!' She still stood there.

'All's fair in love,' he tossed, quite reckless now, 'and it's only when a man has money in his pocket that he can *really* consider love.'

'You never needed it with me,' she cried, 'I always told you so, Kip.'

'Who said,' he came back cuttingly, 'I was speaking about you?'

'What do you mean, Kip——?'

'No, my sweet, *too* sweet innocent, you'd be as much use to me as a bunch of flowers. You're too soft, too vulnerable, too sentimental over things that don't matter. In fact you'd suit his Nibs perfectly, poor fool with his blind mare.' Kip snorted. 'Oh, no, the man who wants to get on, who *will* get on, wants someone steelier than that.'

'No doubt you have someone in view,' she said coldly.

'Oh, I have,' he grinned.

'But when we went to the gem valley and I found the grass stone——'

'I sold it. Not much, but I needed all help for my kill at the Plate.'

'Well, at least you didn't have it set instead for her,' said Paddy hollowly, not believing any of this. 'I suppose it's her.'

'Anthea?'

'Yes.'

'Then yes. No, I didn't, the lady likes diamonds, and will have diamonds, but don't tell David that. Not yet.'

'I will. I'll tell him that you——'

'I don't think so. Because, my dear, when it comes to basics, you're much more involved yourself. I only came here out of natural curiosity. David, as a horse bloke, will understand that. But my God, he won't understand you making it easy for me by passing over a key. He'll think: "*He* went because he's vitally concerned, but why did *she* make it possible for him?" He won't like the answer he arrives at ... and neither will you.'

'You're loathsome, Kip!' she ground out.

'Yet I've done nothing ... except lead you on, and actually you asked quite urgently for it, you know. No' ... catching at Paddy's raised hand ... 'none of that, please. Leave me untouched as I've left your nag untouched.' He nodded back to the horse. 'Be thankful at least for that. Down in the city now ...' His voice trailed away.

Into the Light certainly looked untouched, looked as glossy and beautiful as ever, and the next morning at the trial the horse galloped perfectly, and Paddy, though still smarting, though still hurt and ashamed and belittled, was encouraged enough to try to put the whole wretched thing, and Kip, and Anthea, right out of her mind.

Then the third morning, exactly four days before the Plateau Plate, the lovely animal was reported seedy.

'Nerves?' Magnus asked his vet, for it was well established that highly-bred horses did develop such things.

'No,' frowned Bill Lenehan, 'it's something physical. Yet I've been all over him. Could it be a stomach disagreement?' An estimating pause. 'Any chance of an unwelcome intruder, Magnus?'

Paddy, standing by, heard Magnus reply: 'Every chance, but that simply doesn't happen up here. Anyway, if he had been tampered with you would have seen the evidence earlier, and he would have been far more seedy by now.'

'There are new fiendish tricks,' the vet shrugged. 'The big city studs are beginning to experience them. No immediate sign and slower progression. Not always does the strapper open up in the morning to the shock of finding a prone horse, nowadays it's often more insidious than that.'

'You mean our boy could still be for it?'

'No, I don't, Magnus, I still believe it's only some disagreement.'

But the next day Into the Light was worse, and on the day before the Plateau Plate the lovely acorn creature lay down, sighed, then died.

CHAPTER FOURTEEN

WHY was it that something that never had been able to speak to you, convey thoughts to you, except for a soft nuzzling nose touch you, hurt you so much when it wasn't there any more? *Ever* any more? That was the ache of it all for Paddy and the boys. Into the Light had gone into the dark, he would never be there any more.

They all knew as large a pain as though he had been

human, a kind of amputation of love itself, the futility, the utter uselessness of it left them hollow and burningly dry-eyed. They were too distressed for words. With people, Paddy thought for her stricken four, you could look up at a star and feel a comfort, a sort of comprehension, but with an animal, an animal simply was gone.

She wished desperately for tears for them all.

No one told her anything, and by no one she meant Magnus. She had felt sure Magnus would seek her out at once to question her, and she had braced herself. But he never came near. The only fragments she learned were from Richard and Paul, who relayed stable talk every night.

The vet had had a post-mortem on the horse and it was *not* one of those vicious dopes being currently adopted in the city after all, *not* one of the new slow, deadly things they had previously thought.

'And yet he died,' Paddy sighed.

'Yes,' they said.

The next piece of news was that Standen's entry Peerless Prince was scratched.

'But why?' Paddy asked in amazement. 'He would have been a probable winner.' She added: '*Now*.'

'Norris scratched him before he left,' said Richard.

'*Left——?*' she gasped.

'He's gone from Standen, gone from the plateau. The talk' ... Richard put on a confidential face ... 'is that——'

'I don't want to hear any talk,' Paddy reproved.

But with boys who lived every minute in the excitement of horses, she found she had to. She learned that in the case of country races and in this instance the

Plateau Plate, if a particular stud entrant through unforeseen circumstances became a non-starter, a stable mate could take its place.

That set the boys arguing whether Current Issue was as good as Bonny Heather and for that matter were either of them as good as Ponderous Pete. The king is dead, long live the king, Paddy secretly grieved, and yet life had to be lived like this.

She longed to live her own life again, live it normally, serenely, not jerkily, nervously as she was living it now. But she knew she never would until she spoke with Magnus, told him everything. Why didn't he send for her and *ask*?

It was several days before she noticed Anthea had gone.

'Oh, yes,' shrugged Paul, 'the bird flew.'

Instead of reproving him, Paddy asked: 'When?'

'Soon after Kip Norris. Do you reckon they went together?'

'I reckon they didn't,' came in Richard. 'She was after money, and with Peerless Prince scratched she'd never get it out of him.'

'Stop gossiping, stop conjecturing.' But Paddy would have liked to have known herself.

One thing she had decided on, even if she broke a contract, even if Closer Families refused to place her any more—she was leaving here.

There was, after all, nothing to keep her. The boys were comfortably settled, happily settled, and she knew, however else she disliked him, that Magnus David would keep things comfortable and happy for them.

She also believed that Magnus would make no effort to compel her to honour her agreement. After all, he stood to gain by her going away. Paddy had never believed she had any chance of making a claim on poor Jeremy's will, but it would be easier for Magnus if she quietly withdrew. Probably he was intending to discharge her, anyway, tell her she had been tried and found wanting, and it was only the chaotic events of the last few days that had prevented him from doing this. She would have left at once on her own accord, only that the boys, caught up in the fever, were not looking after themselves as they should, so she would see them through the meeting, and then——

Plateau Plate Day dawned as importantly as a day could, almost as though it knew what was to take place ... anyway, it put on all its silks and satins and all its blues and golds.

Paddy, watching through binoculars from her window, fairly goggled at the elegance of the female attire. She had thought of wearing jodphurs herself, but now she mentally took out a new blue crêpe.

Also something had happened to the surrounds of the bush course; instead of trees and grass and little else there were tents set with bunting, stalls set with flags, and actually a band.

She watched the jockeys with disbelief. They had simply donned anything. There were crash helmets, dungarees and actually some shorts. But the Plate event, said Richard breathlessly behind her, would be strictly silk-and-satin formal as befitted an important race.

'Who are we putting in?' Paddy remembered her decision and changed 'we' to 'you'.

'Current Issue,' said Richard evasively, 'or it could be Ponderous Pete or——'

'Or Lightning's Child.' It was John, the impetuous youngest.

'Shut up, junior,' warned Richard.

'Don't talk like that, Richard, and I don't know any Lightning's Child.'

Because of the big event there was no school that day down in the valley. Paddy helped Mrs Dermott pack four cut lunches that they both knew would not be eaten, not with hamburgers and fairy floss there for the buying, then gave the boys final instructions on how to behave.

'No betting,' she said sternly.

'As though we could, with only fifty cents each!'

But four times fifty made two dollars and Paddy knew that they had other ideas. She wondered with their shining boy gone which of the stable contemporaries . . . Current Issue, Bonny Heather, Ponderous Pete and that other one she had never heard of . . . they would choose to lose their money on. She smiled, shrugged and changed into her blue crêpe.

It was fun down at the course. A little wind was whirling tossed-down pieces of paper and stirring up dust that the lush fields never knew they had.

Paddy saw Magnus, not dressed up at all, just a checked shirt with sleeves rolled up and his usual wide hat pushed to the back of his head. If he saw her, he made no sign.

The races came and went, first silence, then a low buzz of interest, then a scream as the winner flew by.

As the time for the Plate approached, Paddy kept glancing to the Yoothamurra Stud. Yoothamurra was the nearest stable to the course, in fact it was only some hundred yards away. She wondered which entrant would be led out.

Still Magnus was taking no interest, not only in her but in his entry. Probably he had left it to the boys; he liked doing things like that.

Then Paddy saw the boys and their choice emerging from the adjoining stables.

It took her quite a long time to recognise the candidate. She knew most of the girls and boys now, knew that Current Issue was a grey, Bonny Heather a bay and Ponderous Pete very dark. But this filly was plain brown. What had the four called this possibility again? Oh, yes, Lightning's Child. Lightning's Child? Paddy frowned. Lightning. Where had she heard that before? Now she remembered. Quick As Lightning, another one-time Cup winner as Big Harry had been, Quick As Lightning who had served blind Melisande. This Lightning's Child was none other than their own Melisande's Girl, the filly Paul had been riding while one of the boys watched over the blind mare. But who was watching now? Paddy narrowed her eyes and counted. She counted four boys. All at once though she was standing in the bright sunshine she felt icy cold. Was *anyone* watching Melisande?

Was anyone watching that cream-eyed mother who never became upset over anything except her baby? When the child did not answer, when the child did not come to her, Melisande was calm no longer, she became a mad thing, running from fence to fence, forgetting her safety antennae that Magnus had said she had, just flinging herself wildly forward as she looked for her progeny. Was she doing that now? Was blind Melisande destroying herself?

Paddy turned and ran.

She was panting painfully as she reached the stables, she had no breath to call out, and anyway, what would have been the use? The entire stud would have been watching the race.

But Melisande could watch nothing, she could only

look blankly from a cream scum and know a nothing world. Paddy ran over to the small paddock. Perhaps she had only *thought* there had been the four boys with Lightning's Child ... with Melisande's Girl ... perhaps one had been left with the blind mare.

But no, Melisande was there, she was alone, and she was cropping peacefully. Evidently she had not realised yet.

Paddy stood near and barely breathed. Anything, she knew, could arouse the mare, set her calling for her baby, and when the baby did not come there would begin that awful, tortured plunging about, that agonised threshing that Magnus had related.

Still Melisande cropped. Then came the roar as the big race began, a much louder roar this time than before, and Melisande flinched. She let out a beckoning whicker.

Paddy climbed on top of the fence.

'I'm here, darling, no panic, your daughter won't be long.'

Melisande backed, then began kicking the ground. Paddy slid off the fence and walked towards her.

'You shouldn't, you know, you should look after yourself, because I've been told you're going to have another. After all, Quick As Lightning's child was getting far too big to be mollycoddled like you molly-coddle. A boy this time, I think, to take Into the Light's place. Now let me touch you, Melisande. There, that's my good little mother.'

Melisande's cream eyes were in Paddy's direction. She was standing quite still. Paddy kept talking ... and talking ...

That was how Magnus found them. Although he knew it was vital he stepped in at once, he paused a moment and looked. Looked at the girl and the blind mare.

Then he went over and put a rope around Melisande and tethered her.

'I don't think you need have bothered,' Paddy objected. 'I think she still has those antennae.'

'No, she has love,' Magnus said.

They stopped there until the boys ... and the filly ... returned in triumph.

'First! It was a romp.' Richard laughed.

'And you'll be romping after I finish with you. I'm not asking who left Melisande unattended because I put the blame on all four.'

'But Magnus, we *won*!'

'What would a win have been if Melisande had mangled herself on a fence? If she'd done the same to Miss Travis who was misguided enough to interfere?'

It was not quite the same as his previous 'No, she has love.' Paddy, blind like the mare now, turned away.

The Plate had been run early. All at once Paddy knew a longing to run herself, run along a beach ... run back a year to last September. So uninvolved, so simple, so— dear. She could do it if she took the mountain track down to the coast.

The stud change room was empty, and she darted in and took some old overalls from the wall. Within minutes she had gone round to the stable and the mount that had previously been allocated to her. Ordinarily Paddy might have hesitated about descending alone— after all, she was still a newchum rider, but all she wanted, all she *had* to have was escape.

She was gone within minutes, and she was sure no one saw her. In ten minutes again she was taking the steep downward bridle track to the coast.

Remember September. She kept on saying it to herself for comfort, for she never had felt more in need of comfort in all her life. Jerry would give it to her ... not really, of course, but she would think of him and the fun they had had and the good companionship.

She was on the flat now, and she gave Donna her head. When they reached Pelican she kept up the northern end, away from Magnus's caretaker. She tethered Donna loosely to give her plenty of cropping, then turned to the wide expanse of beach.

A car was there, and for a moment Paddy paused, preparing herself to take off again. What was a car doing here? Didn't the driver know this was private property? that campers had to apply first?

In all this time Paddy had not recognised the car, and for quite a while after he got out, she did not recognise Magnus.

Then she did, and she went slowly forward. Magnus came as slowly forward to her. They stopped a few paces from each other. Because she could think of nothing else to say Paddy asked: 'Why are you here?'

'It happens to be my beach.'

'Oh, yes, I know that.' When he said nothing, she babbled more than spoke: 'I should know, I've been told often enough, only always in the plural first, always "our" then a quick correction to "my", my beach, my stud, my property, my possession. Of course I would know.' She waited, but still no comment. 'I really meant how did you know I was here?'

'Blue dresses are not usually found on the floor of the strappers' change room, so when they are, and a pair of cleaning overalls taken, it rather suggests that the owner of the dress has borrowed something more suitable for a ride.'

'So you checked Donna and found she was missing?'

Magnus said, 'I also checked for you and found you were missing as well.'

'But why did you come here?'

'Why did you? No, don't search for some evasive answer, I know already. It was "Remember September", wasn't it? You came for comfort from Jeremy.'

'Yes, I did,' she said honestly. 'I needed Jeremy.'

'And have you found him?' His voice was harsh.

'I've only just arrived.'

'Then do you think you'll find him now?'

'Not with you here, Mr David. Jerry would want your taunts and suspicions and dislikes as much as I've wanted them.'

'But you fool, you utter little fool, there were never taunts, suspicions and dislikes, not really, there was only an awful futility, a terrible blankness.'

'Because of your brother?'

'No,' he said, 'because of you. Poor Jerry might have had a short life but at least it was a full one. I face a long life, possibly, but it's empty.'

'Empty, Magnus?'

'Paddy, I was never young like my brother. I told you the family story, but not all. I was with my mother when she died, and her last words were for Jeremy. "Look after Jeremy." If I'd been younger, then the burden wouldn't have weighed so heavily on me—oh, a beloved burden, yes, but still my load. If I'd been older and wiser, I would have realised that my mother didn't mean what I took her to mean.'

'I think you mean *all your days*, Magnus?'

'All my days, all my life, given to Jeremy.'

'And now you resent that?'

'No, never, but I do resent what Jeremy had and I never had ... spring, laughter, a girl running beside him on a beach.'

'So you took it out on that girl?'

'Yes, I did. If I hadn't taken it out on her, I would have taken her to my heart.' He came a step closer. But that was all, one step, and he did not follow it up.

'The moment I first saw you I knew how wrong I was,' he said flatly, 'but I also saw how young you were, a youngness I'd never known. It tore at me, I think it all but killed me. At no time when I read poor Jeremy's letter leaving all his possessions to some girl did I really intend to deprive that girl, but there was a helpless anger in me that I had never known someone in my life, too, to feel that way, to act that way, so—so——' He shrugged.

'So you found who I was, where I was.'

'And brought you here,' he nodded. 'I was going to hurt the girl——'

'You succeeded,' she assured him.

'I was going to belittle her——'

'You did.'

'After which I was going to give her money and let her go.'

'Well?' Paddy waited.

'Well?' He waited, too.

'Well, why didn't you? Or is this the dismissal now?'

'It's up to you now. Do you want that money? Do you want Out?'

'I don't want money and I love this place, but——'

'Yes?'

'But I can't stay here, not with you.'

'... Not even as Jerry's brother?'

'Especially as Jerry's brother, because in all our companionship here, all Jerry's friendships with me, and that in spite of what you think is all it was, you were always Jerry's light, you were always Jerry's ideal.' Then Paddy quoted:

'Maryrose: Remember September? Magnus.' She repeated: '*Magnus*,' then looked at him.

'I'd forgotten that,' Magnus said, and there was a catch in his voice. He turned away.

When he made no move to face her again, Paddy said gently, touched by his distress: 'Anyway, all your days are not blank, Magnus—there's Anthea. Oh, yes, I know she's left, the boys told me, but she'll be back again.'

'No,' he said definitely, 'that would be the last straw. I only ever accepted her out of politeness, but that quality is not very strong in me, *you* know that, and it soon runs out.'

'As she ran out?' probed Paddy.

'Yes.'

'Ran after Kip ... or was it the other way round?'

'I think if you looked into things, which I don't intend doing, you'd find that both of them have gone their separate paths. Norris would be no good to Anthea without money.'

'*You* had money,' said Paddy.

'But no appeal and no prospects—for her. She soon found that out. Good lord, I hardly knew her, and certainly never liked her. She used to visit her grandparents up here, and once when she came to Yoothamurra she met Norris. I suppose it started something. After all, as *you* know, he is good-looking.'

'Was it Kip who—who——'

'Caused Into the Light's death? Yes, yet no. Not at any time did Norris expect the mild depressant which was all he introduced to have such a disastrous result. That came about from an unfortunate individual tendency or allergy in the colt as regarded the drug he gave him. He did kill him in a way, I suppose, but intentionally, no.'

'He's gone, the boys said. Did you report him?'

'Report him, yes, but charge him, no. You see, he had the decency to come forward—I believe he was almost as shocked as we were. He was planning a kill, but not a kill like that. No, no charge, his career was finished and that was punishment enough. Besides——'

'Besides?' asked Paddy.

'He broke whatever it was between you and him before he went. How could I not feel less than anger then?'

'I don't think there was anything, Magnus, not really, and that key——'

'Oh, yes, I know about the key now, know, too, your incredible naïveté. Who else, *who else* could have inspired such an advertisement: "Maryrose: Remember September? Magnus."'

'It was September, a September to be remembered.'

'And now it's a year after. A September to be remembered, too? Or' ... quickly, a little savagely ... 'is that only for the young? For the springtimers?'

'I think you mean—a girl running beside someone on a beach.'

'Yes, I mean that,' Magnus said.

Paddy was thinking of Jerry. '... Race you to the buoy ... last out of the water buys the lunch ...'

'Race you to the rocks!' she heard herself calling. 'Last there——'

She never finished it. He had her in his arms and he

was kissing her. Eyes, ears, hair, neck, throat.

'I love you, Paddy.'

'I love you, Magnus.'

'I've only autumn to offer you ... then winter.'

'Then spring and the whole bit all over again, for it goes on and on, you know. But now it's September ... a September to remember. Remember it, Magnus. Remember it now.' She stood waiting for him.

Somewhere she could have vowed she heard Jerry applauding, saying: 'My nice big brother and my nice old man, what more could I ask?' Then Jerry's dream voice was sliding away. The beach was sliding away. Everything was sliding away in Magnus's tightening grasp.

When his lips pressed down on hers, Paddy knew it would be a September to be remembered. Not: 'Mary-rose: Remember September? Magnus' but: 'Magnus: Remember September? Paddy.'

She would write that out and insert it in a paper, then years ahead show it to her children, to her grand-children, to his grandchildren. Theirs. She pushed closer to him and stopped there.

Theirs. What a wonderful ... *wonderful* ... thought!

In every issue...

Here's what you'll find:

 a complete, full-length romantic novel...illustrated in color.

 exotic travel feature...an adventurous visit to a romantic faraway corner of the world.

 delightful recipes from around the world...to bring delectable new ideas to your table.

 reader's page...your chance to exchange news and views with other Harlequin readers.

 other features on a wide variety of interesting subjects.

Start enjoying your own copies of Harlequin magazine immediately by completing the subscription reservation form.

Not sold in stores!

Harlequin Reader Service
MPO Box 707,
Niagara Falls, N.Y. 14302

In Canada:
649 Ontario St.
Stratford, Ont. N5A 6W2

I wish to subscribe to Harlequin magazine beginning with the next issue. I enclose my check or money order for $9.00 for 12 monthly issues.

NAME_____

ADDRESS_____

CITY_____

STATE/PROV._____ ZIP/POSTAL CODE_____

ROM 2189